NO WAY BACK

(A Carly See FBI Suspense Thriller—Book 2)

Rylie Dark

Rylie Dark

Bestselling author Rylie Dark is author of the SADIE PRICE FBI SUSPENSE THRILLER series, comprising six books (and counting); the MIA NORTH FBI SUSPENSE THRILLER series, comprising six books (and counting); the CARLY SEE FBI SUSPENSE THRILLER, comprising six books (and counting); and the MORGAN STARK FBI SUSPENSE THRILLER, comprising three books (and counting).

An avid reader and lifelong fan of the mystery and thriller genres, Rylie loves to hear from you, so please feel free to visit www.ryliedark.com to learn more and stay in touch.

ISBN: 978-1-0943-9457-2

BOOKS BY RYLIE DARK

SADIE PRICE FBI SUSPENSE THRILLER
ONLY MURDER (Book #1)
ONLY RAGE (Book #2)
ONLY HIS (Book #3)
ONLY ONCE (Book #4)
ONLY SPITE (Book #5)
ONLY MADNESS (Book #6)

MIA NORTH FBI SUSPENSE THRILLER
SEE HER RUN (Book #1)
SEE HER HIDE (Book #2)
SEE HER SCREAM (Book #3)
SEE HER VANISH (Book #4)
SEE HER GONE (Book #5)
SEE HER DEAD (Book #6)

CARLY SEE FBI SUSPENSE THRILLER
NO WAY OUT (Book #1)
NO WAY BACK (Book #2)
NO WAY HOME (Book #3)
NO WAY LEFT (Book #4)
NO WAY UP (Book #5)
NO WAY TO DIE (Book #6)

MORGAN STARK FBI SUSPENSE THRILLER
TOO LATE (Book #1)
TOO CLOSE (Book #2)
TOO FAR GONE (Book #3)

PROLOGUE

Ariana Welch was feeling really happy with the decisions she'd made. As she walked along the well-lit street, she took a long, deep breath of warm, clean night air.

"I'm definitely not in Wisconsin anymore," she whispered aloud

It was early fall, and she didn't even need a jacket here in Teapa, New Mexico. In fact, she could expect the temperature to barely dip below freezing all winter. She actually shivered a little as she imagined what it would be like back in Wisconsin right now, with a damp chill in the air and trees mostly barren of leaves.

After a whole lifetime in in the northern midwest, she'd had enough of the climate and just about everything else about it, and Teapa was a welcome change. Ariana had let her friend and now-roommate Jolene Vaughn talk her into dropping out of the accounting program at the University of Madison to move down here.

Now she was so glad she had. Not that she was entirely sold on some of Jolene's notions about this town—the heart-chakra of the southwest, Jolene called it. Ariana didn't share Jolene's fascination with power centers and crystals and astrology and such, but it wasn't a bone of contention between them. They got along just fine.

Ariana wasn't alarmed to hear footsteps behind her. Even at this hour, it was a safe neighborhood, flanked mostly by art stores and galleries that had closed for the night. But she was a little startled to hear a man's voice call out to her.

"Hey, Ariana!"

She turned and saw a man trotting toward her. He was about her age and wearing a sports jacket and a tie.

"Fancy running into you again," he said, walking alongside her now.

Ariana wasn't sure what to say for a moment. She thought she recognized the guy, but her mind was maybe a little foggy after three Long Island Iced Teas. Then she remembered where she'd seen him. A little while ago at the bar at the Bighorn, he'd tried to strike up a conversation with her. She hadn't been interested, so she'd ignored him and kept right on talking to the bartender. He'd finally wandered away and Ariana thought she'd seen the last of him, at least for tonight.

"Uh, yeah, what a surprise," she said, forcing a smile.

It was the best she could do for a greeting.

"You don't remember my name, I guess," the young man said with a wink. "That's OK, I know I'm not the most memorable guy in the world. My name is Larry. Larry Damon. And I remember all about you. Ariana Welch, the bank teller from Beloit, Wisconsin, looking for a change here in wonderful Teapa, New Mexico."

Ariana felt an uneasy twinge.

How much did I tell him about myself, anyway? She wondered.

All she remembered from the conversation was that she'd been glad to get it over with. She may have babbled a bit just to get rid of him, and the drinks might have loosened her tongue.

"So where are you headed?" Larry said.

"Home."

"Oh? Where do you live?"

Ariana almost blurted out the name of her street, but quickly thought better of it. After all, it was kind of a pushy question, and Larry Damon seemed like kind of a pushy guy. She felt like maybe he knew too much about her already.

She decided the best thing was to say nothing at all.

So she looked away from him and walked in silence as if he weren't there. Her silence felt awkward. She felt as though she was being awfully rude—although maybe not as rude as if she'd blurted out what she really thought.

"Where I live is none of your business."

The guy kept walking beside her with his hands in his pockets.

Finally, he said, "It's kind of late, you know. Maybe you'd feel safer if I walked you home."

"No thanks, I'll be fine."

"Are you sure?"

"I'm sure."

More than sure, she thought.

In fact, she was starting to feel a bit anxious now, and she wondered how she was going to shake this guy off. Then an idea occurred to her. She took out her cellphone and acted as though she was about to make a phone call.

Maybe he'll think I'm calling the police, she thought.

The man quickly pointed to a side street.

"Well, I'm headed over this way. You have a nice night."

"You too."

Larry Damon turned and walked away.

It worked, she thought with a smile.

She was glad she hadn't had to resort more desperate measures, like pepper spray, screaming for help, her self-defense training, or actually calling the police. But she doubted things would have come to that, even if she hadn't shaken him off so easily.

He'd seemed harmless enough—just annoying and a little creepy.

Ariana soon came to her own street and turned to the right. It was a quiet little street lined with houses instead of shops. She took her keys out of her purse as she approached her own address. She knew Jolene would be out all night with her new boyfriend and not here to answer the door.

As she walked up onto the front stoop, Ariana heard a scuffling sound behind her. Before she could whirl around, someone seized one arm and forced it painfully behind her back.

Then a hand clapped a damp rag over her nose and mouth.

Ariana gasped, inhaling sharply and reflexively. The startlingly sweet taste and odor seemed coolly antiseptic, like a hospital hallway.

She wasn't conscious long enough to get scared. Her head buzzed with what seemed to be white noise and television snow.

Then everything went black.

CHAPTER ONE

Carly See hoped she didn't look as nervous as she felt. She had something momentous to say, but she had no idea how to go about saying it. And here in her parents' living room, she had to struggle against feeling like the self-conscious child she had once been. Maybe the problem was that stern, expectant look on her mother's face, or perhaps it was that detached expression on Dad's face that told her he was already a bit bored.

She sternly reminded herself that she was 30 years old with a successful FBI career. She even looked the part, wearing nice slacks and a jacket with her dark hair neatly confined in a bun at the back of her neck.

"So, what are you so anxious to talk to us about?" Mom asked.

"Yeah," Dad grumbled, looking at his watch. "It's late. Your mother and I both have to work tomorrow."

Carly swallowed down a hard knot of anxiety.

How can I explain it to them? she wondered.

Her parents had picked her up at the airport after her flight from Washington, D.C. She was on leave from the Behavioral Analysis Unit after suffering a shoulder wound during her most recent murder case. After recuperating for a boring week in her apartment, now had seemed like a good time to pay an overdue visit to her family in Currie, Illinois.

Carly had hinted to her parents during the drive home from the airport that she had something urgent to discuss with them.

Maybe that wasn't such a good idea, she thought.

Mom drummed her fingers on the arm of the Chesterfield sofa where she and Dad were sitting.

"I hope you're going to tell us you're quitting that awful job of yours," she said. "Are you going back to school, maybe? Please say yes. Because you know, I think you're wasting lots of great academic potential."

An English professor at a local community college, Mom still harbored dreams of Carly becoming a renowned scholar at some big university, achieving the kind of success she herself had never had.

Very carefully, Carly set her cup of steaming hot chocolate into its saucer on the nearby end table. She silently congratulated herself on not spilling a drop on the carpet.

"That's not it, Mom."

"Then what is it? Are you getting married or something? Don't tell us you've eloped. That would be really foolish."

Then Mom gasped.

"Oh, please don't say you've gotten pregnant. That would be just awful. You mustn't do *anything* to limit your possibilities in life. No more than you already have, anyway. You're not getting any younger, you know."

Carly felt her teeth grinding. She didn't feel as though life was passing her by. Far from it: she loved her work and the life she lived.

"Maybe now's not the time. Maybe it'll wait till morning."

"No, it won't," Mom said. "You've got us in suspense. Out with it now."

That seems only fair, Carly thought.

She spoke slowly and haltingly.

"Mom … Dad … do you ever think about … Megan?"

Dad let out a groan of annoyance.

A hurt look crossed Mom's brow.

"Why, we think about your sister every day, dear. She'll always be part of our family, and we'll always love her. How can we help it? I don't think you're being very sensitive. Why on earth are you asking such a thing?"

That's a good question, Carly thought.

She wished she could just say, *"Never mind, just forget I said anything about her."*

But she'd taken an irrevocable step just by mentioning the name of her younger sister, an all-but-forbidden topic here at home. Megan had been 18 when she'd gone missing, and Carly had been 20. That had been some 10 years ago, and Megan had never been seen since then.

Still speaking cautiously, Carly continued.

"What I mean is … do you ever wonder … ?"

Carly's voice faded. Dad finished her thought with a growl in his voice.

"If she's still alive? No, we don't. She's dead. She's even been officially, legally dead for several years now. We don't know how she died, but we've long since made our peace about that. We'll never know."

"Now, Russell—" Mom began.

But Dad talked right over her to Carly.

"And don't tell me you've got some reason to think otherwise. Because if Megan is still alive somewhere …"

Dad's voice suddenly choked off.

Carly knew what he was leaving unsaid. If Megan was still alive, it had been unbelievably cruel of her to disappear from all their lives for so many years with no explanation. In some horrible way, it hurt less for Dad to suppose Megan was dead, even if she might have met some awful fate.

Dad pulled himself upright and said, "Enough of this. I'm going to watch TV for a while, and then I'm going to bed."

He got up from his chair and said to Carly in an almost sarcastic tone, "Welcome home, sweetheart."

Dad walked away and disappeared toward his den.

Mom shook her head.

"Oh, it's always the TV. He spends his every spare hour sitting in front of that thing. I'm surprised he even deigned to sit down with us for a few minutes. I swear, I sometimes wonder why I ever married that man. Lord only knows he doesn't understand the first thing about me."

Carly's mouth soured at the familiar note of resentment in Mom's voice.

Mom was a great hoarder of grudges and grievances. She made no secret of blaming Dad for the fact that she was stuck in this town living such an insufferably dull life.

But Dad was a local dentist, and a pretty successful one at that, and Carly knew perfectly well that Mom had done a thorough cost-benefit analysis before she'd married him. Dad wasn't really to blame for their dismal marriage, and Carly couldn't help sympathizing with his need to cut himself off emotionally.

I just wish he wouldn't cut himself off from me, she thought.

Mom took a sip of cocoa.

"But why are you bringing up Megan out of the blue like this? I don't understand."

Carly swallowed hard.

"I just wondered—have you and Dad heard anything from her at all?"

"Of course not. Don't you think we would have told you if we had?"

A silence fell. Watching Mom closely, Carly was aware of the resemblance between them. Her mother's dark hair was beginning to show some gray, and she wore it in a more stylish cut than Carly's, but the oval face, dark eyebrows, and determined expression were similar.

"Have *you* heard something from her?" Mom asked anxiously

Carly felt her hands shaking now.

"Not exactly *from* her …"

"Then something *about* her?" Mom asked, her voice shaking with emotion.

Carly gulped hard and nodded slightly.

Mom stammered, "Do you—do you think she's alive?"

"I think—I think maybe so."

Mom gasped and her eyelids widened.

"Tell me."

Carly took a long, deep breath.

Now for the hard part, she thought.

Carly spoke very slowly.

"Mom, we've never talked about this, but … I sometimes get these …"

Carly fell silent.

Mom leaned toward her and whispered, "Messages? Communications?"

Carly's eyes widened with surprise. This was hardly the reaction she had expected.

"Why—yes. How—how did you know?"

"Carly, I got the feeling back when you were a little girl that there was something unusual about you. I didn't want to pay attention. There had always been … rumors … about my grandmother. She was given to 'seeing' weird things. I never wanted to believe it and certainly didn't want anything like that in my own family."

Carly had never heard that, and she had no idea what to say.

"But she had those big gray eyes," Mom murmured. "Just like you."

Carly just stared into her mother's steely blue eyes. Finally she asked, "What made you suspect that I … ?"

"Do you remember when that little boy went missing all those years ago? Tyler Glick was his name."

"I remember."

Indeed, she remembered all too well. She and Tyler had been friends all through childhood. But when she and Tyler were both 12, Tyler had left school one day and never got home. No one had any idea what had happened to him or where to look for him.

Then one night, Carly had a dream about a pinwheel—a toy pinwheel Tyler had given her as a party gift at his seventh birthday party. The pinwheel was huge in her dream, and it changed shape into a wind-powered water-pump with a whirling, multi-bladed wheel at the top of a tower. She'd dreamed that Tyler was lying motionless on the ground nearby.

Mom continued, "You told me you thought Tyler was near the windmill on Mercer's farm. You didn't say why you thought that, but you were most insistent about it, and finally I finally got Sheriff Corcoran to look there, and that's where …"

Mom's voice faded, but Carly knew what she was leaving unsaid.

That's where they found Tyler's body.

Then Mom said, "The truth was, I hoped it was just a one-time thing, so I never told you about Grammie. And years passed, and you never mentioned anything like that again. I figured either you'd outgrown it, or I'd been wrong and you'd never had it to begin with. But now …"

Mom stared hard at Carly for a moment.

"How do you know your sister is alive?"

Carly shook her head.

"Mom, I'm not sure I *know* anything. And it's not like I've gotten any messages directly from Megan. I only get messages from dead people. But I heard Tyler speaking in a dream, and he showed me Megan, and she was alive—or at least she looked alive. She was standing on a beach."

"What beach? Where is it?"

"I don't know."

"You mean you didn't ask Tyler?"

Carly stifled a groan of despair.

"Mom, it doesn't work like that at all. Messages come to me in hints and riddles. Sometimes they don't make any sense. It's never easy, and I don't have any control over them at all."

Mom's voice was shaking now.

"If your sister is alive, it's up to you to find her."

"But Mom—"

"It's up to you, I said. And if you're not getting any more mysterious messages about it, you've got to find her some other way. Now that you know she's alive, that should be easy for you. You're in the FBI. You should be able to find anybody anywhere."

Carly lowered her eyes from her mother's face. Now she wished she'd never brought this up at all. How could she begin to tell Mom how hard she'd tried to track Megan down, long before this recent communication? She'd used every resource available to her as a BAU agent. She hadn't been able to find a trace of her missing sister. She'd actually supposed she was dead—at least until that recent dream.

"Mom, it's not that simple."

Mom sat staring at Carly for a long moment.

Then she said, "I'm sorry. I didn't mean to snap at you. But the truth is, I don't even know why you bothered to come home if this is all you've got to say. I just don't understand."

Mom got up from her chair and collected the empty cups and saucers.

"I'm going to clean things up and go to bed. You should do that too."

Mom disappeared into the kitchen. Carly heaved a long, weary sigh and got up from the chair. She went and peeked into the den, where Dad was watching some old sitcom on TV. She thought about going in and kissing him goodnight or at least saying something to him. But she quickly thought better of it.

Why did I bring Megan up? she wondered as she climbed the stairs to her old bedroom. She felt exhausted and realized that she could definitely use some sleep herself.

But what am I even doing here?

CHAPTER TWO

Toby Higgins blinked with surprise. The woman sprawled on the grass in Cottage Grove Park was lying in an odd position. And she wasn't moving.

Toby and his German Shepherd, Jupiter, were out for their routine early morning walk along the park's pedestrian pathways. As usual, Jupiter kept tugging aggressively on his leash.

"Not so fast, boy," Toby said, pulling him back.

But Jupiter kept right on pulling.

Toby tugged again and spoke more sharply, "Stay."

This time Jupiter stopped pulling and looked up as if to ask what he was supposed to do next.

"Good boy," Toby told his dog, pleased that the obedience lessons were being effective. Then he moved closer to the low-lying iron fence that separated the grass from the path and stared at the figure. She was ten feet or more beyond the fence, and she'd ignored a DON'T WALK ON THE GRASS sign when she chose that spot.

"Performance art," a voice beside him commented.

Toby realized that he wasn't the only passerby who had noticed the woman. Four other people had gathered to look at her. Others who kept walking along hesitated long enough to gawk, point, and laugh.

Teapa was an art town, and performance art was becoming so common that people were getting to be kind of jaded with it. Recently he'd seen a nearly naked woman lying motionless on a gallery floor, twisted and still as patrons oohed and ahhed and stepped around her, nodding to each other and making sage comments about what the performance's hidden meaning must be.

But there had been a proliferation of outdoor acts during the summer, to the point where you ran into some kind of odd, artsy behavior almost every day. Yesterday a group of dancers had performed as though they were marionettes, creating an illusion so powerful that Toby could almost see the nonexistent strings that "controlled" their movements.

But he'd been most impressed by last week's "human statue" who managed to hold difficult poses for astonishing long intervals without any visible movement. He thought that must be what this woman was doing today, although lying down must make it easier.

A couple of other onlookers called out snidely to the woman.

"You're not very good at this, lady."

"Don't quit your day job."

To her credit, the woman didn't show even the slightest trace of a reaction.

She looks pretty good at it to me, Toby thought.

The pose was a weird one, though. With her right arm reaching forward and her left leg stretched back with the toe pointed, it didn't look like a position she could hold for more than a few minutes.

Toby asked one of the watchers, "How long has she been doing this?"

The man shrugged.

"I dunno. I guess she was already out here when people started coming by early this morning."

Toby felt a tingle of uneasiness now. Something didn't seem right about this particular performance. For one thing, the woman was wearing perfectly ordinary clothes, not a costume.

What kind of a statement is she trying to make? Toby wondered.

He heard Jupiter whine and looked down to see that his dog was staring through the fence. Jupiter seemed anxious to leave the path and go over to the woman on the grass.

Toby tried to shake off his worry and get on with his morning.

"Let's go, boy," Toby said, starting to walk away.

But Jupiter wouldn't come with him. He began to shuffle agitatedly back and forth in front of the low fence.

Toby squinted at the prone woman, feeling worried now.

Maybe I'd better check this out, he thought.

He slacked up on the leash, and Jupiter hopped over the low fence. Toby followed behind him.

One of the watchers called out with a laugh, "Hey, can't you read the sign?"

Another complained, "Leave her alone; you're going to ruin her act."

Toby ignored them and continued over to where the woman was sprawled in her peculiar pose. Then he saw how she was managing to stay in that position. A gray mound of what looked like clay supported her head. Two more gray mounds held her arm and leg in place.

So that's how she stays so still, he thought.

Then Jupiter suddenly poked his nose on the woman's left elbow, but she still didn't budge.

As Toby watched closely, he couldn't even see any sign of her breathing.

His own breathing was getting unsteady now.

This is more than just good concentration, he thought.

Then he laughed nervously.

Now I get it.

Surely this wasn't a person at all, but some sort of detailed mannequin. He walked around to get a better look at the figure's face.

For a moment Toby felt relieved. The face did seem weirdly masklike, waxy and pale. The hairline had been shaved back above her forehead and the eyes were closed. Even so, Toby could see that the skin was porous—and real.

This was no mannequin.

With a whine, Jupiter poked his nose against the woman's cheek. Nothing about the face changed—not so much as a flutter of an eyelid.

Something's really wrong with her, Toby thought.

Then he recalled how a woman's body had been found a couple of days ago right near here. An awful realization seized Toby, and he staggered back a few steps with a loud cry. As he struggled to keep from falling to the ground, he realized that people on the walkway were staring at him now.

"Someone call 911," he shouted. "She's dead."

CHAPTER THREE

Carly hesitated before turning the doorknob to enter her sister's bedroom.

The sign on the door said:

KNOCK BEFORE ENTERING

That sign had hung there ever since she and Megan were teenagers. Carly could remember ignoring the warning just once back then, and she also remembered the screaming adolescent tantrum Megan had thrown about it. She'd respected her sister's privacy after that.

It still feels like I ought to knock first, Carly thought.

But if she did, of course, no one was going to answer—not anymore.

Even on her infrequent visits home, Carly had seldom been inside her sister's bedroom. Once, years ago, she'd entered in a vain search for any sign from the sister she presumed to be dead. But Carly had learned early on that the dead didn't necessarily respond to her call, so the lack of results hadn't been shocking.

Carly wasn't at all sure what she hoped to find out now. But she had to give this a try, and this morning was the best time to go in there. Mom and Dad had gone off to work before Carly had awakened. She had gotten up and dressed and fixed herself toast and coffee for breakfast. Now she had the house to herself and wouldn't have to answer any questions about why she was poking around in Megan's room.

Carly cautiously turned the doorknob and pushed open the door and stopped breathing for a moment at what she saw.

The room was filled by an otherworldly glow from the morning sunlight slanting in through the window. As she stepped inside, Carly felt as though she'd been transported back in time. Even the posters of Megan's male teenage pop idols were still hanging on the wall, and her desk was neatly arranged as if she might have homework to do after school today.

There wasn't a speck of dust in sight, not even afloat in the beaming sunlight. Which meant, of course, that Mom had never stopped taking care of this room, cleaning and dusting and always keeping it exactly as Megan had left it, as if she might return at any time. For a long moment Carly had the strange feeling that a youthful Megan still haunted this timeless place.

But she was yanked abruptly back to the present at the sight of her own reflection in the mirror on the dresser. She saw no trace of the confused and shy youngster who had grown up in this house. This was her own mature face, wide gray eyes beneath dark brows, and full, serious lips. Normally tied back, her long black hair was hanging free today.

And in the present time, Megan had been gone for many years.

As she had before, Carly wondered—had her sister meant to leave for good? She'd taken nothing with her. She hadn't packed for a trip or taken extra money out of her bank account. She hadn't even taken her most treasured possession, a water globe with two frolicking dolphins inside. Instead of the fake snow found in ordinary snow globes, the dolphins were engulfed in whirling bubbles.

Looking at it now, Carly remembered what Megan had said about the scene contained in that globe.

"It's my secret place."

Megan would spend long minutes at a time staring raptly into the globe, as if she wanted to join the dolphins in their aquatic ballet.

And maybe that's what she finally did.

Maybe she went looking for her dolphins.

Carly flashed back to the vision that had brought her back home in the first place—her glimpse of Megan standing on a beach at the edge of the surf looking out over the ocean at a golden sunset. Megan was no longer the teenager she'd been when she'd disappeared, but a woman nearly Carly's age, looking like Megan would look if she were still alive.

The vision had been the first hint Carly had gotten in all these years that Megan might still be alive. Although that had come to her as a message from her dead childhood friend, Tyler had been silent since then. Alone now in Megan's room, she hoped to get a similar insight—something more specific and informative.

Of course, she knew she wasn't going to be able to communicate *directly* with Megan—at least not if Megan was alive. Her earlier vision of Megan on the beach had come to her by way of the spirit of their deceased childhood friend, Tyler.

"I came here just to show you something," Tyler had said before he'd shown her the scene.

She picked up the water globe and sat down in an antique rocking chair.

She gave the globe a shake, making it look as though the dolphins were leaping and dancing. Rocking herself gently, she closed her eyes, trying to visualize the scene at the beach again.

But nothing came.

Carly groaned and rotated her shoulder, which was still sore from the knife wound she'd received on her last case. She wondered if maybe it was the pain that was distracting her.

"Tyler, are you there?" she murmured aloud. "Can you help me find Megan?"

There was still no reply.

After a minute or two of failed effort, she opened her eyes and looked at the water globe still cradled in her hands. The bubbles had settled down and the dolphins no longer appeared to be dancing, and Carly didn't bother to shake the globe again.

A familiar frustration crept over her. She wondered as she often did—what was the point in being able to connect with the dead? How could it possibly be a "gift"? Even at their best, the messages came in hints and riddles, seldom as anything forthright and coherent, and she sometimes found herself unable to make any sense of them.

Almost as if the beyond is taunting me, she thought.

Not that her gift never proved to be useful. To the contrary, it had definitely helped in her law enforcement work. She couldn't count the number of times a spirit had reached out to her and offered hints that made it possible to solve some sort of a homicide case.

Of course, she couldn't tell anybody about these communications—not even her trusted partner, mentor, and friend Lyle Ramsey. She always had to make it look as though she worked things out solely through ordinary investigative methods.

Ever since Tyler had appeared in that vision, she'd wondered whether maybe now, at long last, she could use her gift for her own sake, and for the sake of people she loved.

If that was so, why was she coming up with nothing right now—not even a flicker of communication from Tyler or anybody else's spirit?

Maybe I was wrong, she thought with a despairing sigh.

For all she really knew, Tyler's "communication" had been nothing more than a product of her imagination. Indeed, she sometimes did mistake her own fantasies and musings for genuine communications.

Maybe that's what happened this time.

Maybe Megan isn't even really alive at all.

Maybe it was even wrong of Carly to hope otherwise.

She gave the globe another shake but this time the bubbles looked just like ordinary bubbles, and the dolphins like nothing more than plastic toys.

I shouldn't have come home, she thought.

Then again, she could think of one good thing that had come of her visit. Until last night, Mom had never told her she wasn't the first woman in the family to have her strange ability. Carly wished she'd known her great-grandmother, who had died before she was born.

Maybe Grammie could have told me what my gift is good for, she thought.

Maybe then Carly wouldn't feel so alone.

Meanwhile, Carly could only hope that she could iron things out with her parents during the few days she planned to be here. But the truth was, she seldom really enjoyed their company, and they didn't seem to enjoy hers. They were both bitter, unhappy people, and although Carly felt sorry for them, there was nothing she could do to fix their lives.

After just one night here, she more than half-wished she was on her way back to her apartment in Glensted, Virginia.

Her thoughts were interrupted by the sound of the doorbell.

Carly was startled. Surely everyone who lived here in Currie knew that her parents would both be at work at this time of morning.

So who could that be?

CHAPTER FOUR

The doorbell rang again as Carly dashed downstairs.

When she opened the door, it took her a moment to recognize the visitor. It was a face she hadn't seen for many years—although she had once known it well.

"Hi, Mark," she said.

"Hi, Carly."

His face was fuller now. There were darker circles beneath his eyes, and more furrows in his brow. And he was wearing glasses. Even so, Mark Lawson still had the same earnest good looks that he'd had a decade ago.

"How did you know I was here?" Carly asked.

"Hey, this is Currie, Illinois."

Carly chuckled a little. She'd almost forgotten how fast word traveled here. Doubtless Mom had mentioned her arrival to a student or fellow teacher, or Dad had said something to his dental assistant or his receptionist or one of his patients, and in maybe less than an hour almost everyone in Currie had known she was in town.

As a result of that, her high school sweetheart was standing here at her parent's front door. She and Mark had gone off to separate colleges but had kept in touch for a while. And then their lives had suddenly diverged.

Carly felt tongue-tied, and she could see that Mark was also groping for what to say next.

"Would you like to come in for a cup of coffee?" Carly finally blurted.

He looked at his watch and shuffled his feet.

"Naw, I'd better not. I've got an appointment with a client in just a little while."

Then he added with a wink, "I'm a big city lawyer now, in case you didn't know."

Indeed, Carly did know that Mark had a tiny law firm, which was nevertheless probably the biggest one in Currie.

She nodded toward the porch swing.

"Well, let's sit down for a minute, anyway."

"Yeah, let's do that."

When they sat down together on the porch swing, its chains creaked noisily. Carly wondered how often Mom or Dad ever sat here anymore—or whether they did at all.

Probably not together, she thought.

They were both silent for a moment. Carly found it both strange and bittersweet to be sitting together swaying slightly on that swing as a pleasant autumn breeze wafted by. It stirred memories she hadn't thought of for a long while.

Mark finally broke the shy silence between them.

"So—how's your life been?"

Carly chuckled again.

"Well, since everybody in Currie knows everything about everybody who ever lived here, I guess you know I'm an FBI agent now."

"Yeah, so I heard. You're with the BAU, right?"

"Right."

"That must be pretty intense. How's it working out for you?"

"Oh, it's, you know …"

Carly fell silent for a moment as she tried to think about how to answer that question. But there was one thing she could honestly say.

"It's rewarding."

"Still single?"

Carly rolled her eyes and shook her head with a smile.

"Oh, yeah. It's the kind of work that … well, you don't want to bring home to someone you care about. It's like you said—pretty intense. How about you?"

Mark shrugged wearily, as if he were carrying some sort of heavy load.

"I guess you heard that Judy and I got divorced a couple of years back."

Indeed, Mom had informed her of the breakup in one of their infrequent phone calls.

"Yeah, I heard. I'm sorry."

"Oh, don't be. Judy got awfully bored with life here in Currie, and to tell the truth … she got awfully bored with me. Worse than that, she said I was 'all closed off.' And I guess she was right. I'm just glad we didn't have any children."

Children, Carly thought wistfully.

She couldn't even imagine such a thing in her own life.

Another silence fell.

Carly's hands fidgeted, as if she didn't know what to do with them.

She quickly realized—even after all these years, it felt a little odd that she and Mark weren't holding hands while sitting here. Their typically torrid teenage make-out sessions had taken place elsewhere, usually in the back of Mark's car, and the hours they'd spent sitting here on the porch had been sweet and almost childlike, filled with talk about the future.

Carly felt a twinge of sadness as she remembered the hopes and dreams that they'd shared. Although her interest in law enforcement had already been piqued by Tyler's murder, those plans had still been vague when she and Mark were dating. She'd fantasized about traveling to faraway places, and she loved to talk to Mark about real and imaginary foreign lands.

For Mark's part, he dreamed of becoming a famous author and writing "the great American novel." She couldn't remember him once mentioning any desire to be a small-town lawyer.

How many of our dreams came true? Carly wondered.

Very few, she supposed—especially not their expectations of getting married and raising kids and spending their lives together.

Somehow, Megan's disappearance had disrupted every one of those dreams.

As Carly's sister and Mark's good friend, Megan had spent a lot of time with them. In fact, Mark had even taken the very last photograph of Carly's sister that she knew of—a happy snapshot of Megan and Carly eating cotton candy at a carnival together.

But then came that summer day when Megan inexplicably disappeared, neither the police nor her parents had been able to find a trace of her. Both Carly and Mark had called everyone they knew, had looked everywhere they could think of, to no avail.

She and Mark had broken up soon afterwards. They hadn't really talked about why, and probably didn't even know why at the time. But looking back, Carly now realized she and Mark had come to remind each other of happier times with Megan. It had become impossible for them not to be sad whenever they were together.

Mark cleared his throat and said, "It's uh, nice, to see you again. It's been a long time."

"Yes, it has been. And I'm glad you came by."

With a bit of surprise, she realized that she meant those words. There was something very pleasant about being here with this grown-up man who had been such an important part of her earlier life.

Then she wondered—how would Mark feel if she told him she'd gotten some hint that maybe, just maybe, Megan *might* be alive? Might it make him feel just a bit better? Might it even bring the two of them closer together again?

Maybe, but she couldn't imagine how to break it to him. Even during all their talks together years ago, she'd never told him about her gift. She'd never told a single soul anything about that.

And yet ...

How would this mature Mark take it if she told him now? Couldn't she at least drop some sort of a hint?

Her thoughts were interrupted by the sound of her phone buzzing. Her breath quickened to see she'd gotten a text message from her partner, Special Agent Lyle Ramsey.

"Let's talk soon," the message said.

"Anything important?" Mark asked.

"Uh, it's just my partner."

Mark looked at his watch as he got up from the porch swing.

"Sounds like you'd better get back to him. I've got to get going myself."

He handed a business card to Carly.

"Let's not be strangers, OK? Give me a call sometime. Maybe we can get together before you leave town."

Carly felt a stab of sadness as she watched Mark walk off the front porch and continue on his way.

Will we see each other again? she wondered. *Should we?*

Carly didn't know, and right now she wanted to call Lyle.

"Hey, kid, how are you doing?" her partner said when he answered her call.

"OK, I guess."

But the truth was, the short time she'd spent in Currie hadn't exactly been relaxing.

"What's going on with you?" Carly asked.

"Oh, nothing you need to worry about. I just thought I'd keep you in the loop. I'm on a flight right now, heading off to sunny New Mexico on a case. I don't know much about it yet, but it might be another serial. There have been two victims so far."

"Are you doing the case solo?" Carly asked with slight surprise.

"I wish. But naw, they'd never let me do that. They're hooking me up with somebody from the Albuquerque field office. I hope it's somebody worth a damn, not some rookie who doesn't know what he's doing, or some old-timer counting the hours to retirement. I'll let you know how things go."

Carly squinted her eyes with thought.

"Are you sure you don't want me to—?"

"Carly, don't even think about it. You've been through a traumatic experience. You're recovering from a knife wound. You need to rest. And you're still on leave."

"Actually, I'm feeling OK."

"Good. Keep feeling that way. And enjoy spending some time with your family."

Lyle's words brought Carly up short.

Enjoy spending time with my family?

There didn't seem to be much chance of that.

"Lyle, where can I meet you?" Carly blurted.

"Carly—"

"Lyle, I'm coming to New Mexico, and I'm working the case with you, whether you like it or not. Now are you going to make it hard for me to track you down, or are you just going to tell me where I can meet you?"

Lyle heaved a long sigh. But it didn't sound like a sigh of resignation to Carly. It sounded more like a sigh of relief that the two of them would be working as a team, as usual.

"OK, I'll meet you at the Albuquerque Airport. We'll drive from there to Teapa, where the murders happened. Just let me know your arrival information as soon as you get something booked."

They ended the call, and Carly sat staring at the phone for a moment, wondering whether she'd made the right decision. But then she remembered her mother's words from the night before.

"I don't even know why you bothered to come home ..."

The truth was, Carly didn't feel like she knew either.

Carly immediately started looking for flight information on her cellphone.

It'll feel good to be doing something useful, she thought.

CHAPTER FIVE

Carly still fell a little dazed. The last couple of hours had been a whirl of frantic activity, and now she was looking out over midwestern farmland as the plane droned southwest into another time zone.

After she'd booked her flight to Albuquerque, she'd called Mom and Dad to let them know she was catching a cab to Downing Peoria International Airport and was on her way to work on a new case. She wasn't surprised that neither one of them seemed especially distraught about her sudden departure.

Both of their responses had been pretty much monosyllabic.

"Come back again soon," Dad had said, not exactly in a heartfelt manner.

"I hope you have a nice trip, dear," Mom had said.

There had actually been a note of hardness in Mom's voice. Carly realized that her mother was a bit bitter after their last conversation.

I should never have mentioned Megan, she thought yet again.

Carly knew that by now Mom was probably pretending that their conversation hadn't even happened.

But what was done was done. Dressed in slacks and a jacket with her hair pulled back in a bun, Carly felt like a BAU agent again today, and not an out-of-place small-town girl. It was good to be getting back on the job.

She did feel one regret. She'd texted Mark that she had to hurry off on another case and wouldn't be getting together with him after all.

His response had made her smile.

"I understand. Good hunting."

It had been short and sweet and oddly thoughtful, and it made Carly happy that she'd seen Mark at least for a few minutes. And now she found herself musing about those words his ex-wife had chosen to describe him.

"All closed off."

She was sure people said the same thing about her. And the truth was, she had no great desire to change that. She was more comfortable keeping some aspects of her life private.

Something Mark and I have in common, I guess, she thought.

Those words kept rattling through Carly's head.

All closed off.

Here they were, two lonely "closed off" people who once shared magical feelings for one another. She could remember when she and Mark had been anything but closed off to each other. During their high school and college years, she'd felt closer to him than to anyone, other than Megan.

Megan's shocking disappearance had ended those days for both of them.

It even changed who Mark and I are today, she realized.

But now she couldn't help but wonder—might two "closed off" people understand each other especially well, and even be good for each other? Of course, it was hard to imagine how a BAU agent and a small-town lawyer could make a life together.

And yet ... at least we should try to stay in touch, she decided.

Meanwhile, it was time for her to get her mind on the upcoming case, so she took out her computer tablet. Before she'd left Peoria, she'd downloaded some police files about the two murders in Teapa, New Mexico. Now she opened up those files to look at photographs of the two victims.

Although these were far from the grisliest crime scene photos she'd ever seen, they were odd enough to be unsettling. She was glad no one was seated next to her as she studied them.

The cause of death for last night's victim was yet to be officially determined, but it seemed likely that it was the same as the first one.

Gemma Gosnell had died of suffocation. Two days ago, her body had been found on the bank of a stream in a public park. The police had been called to the scene by an early-morning jogger who had tried to wake up a woman she thought might be sleeping or ill. The photos showed the corpse lying face up on the ground, with her hands on her hips. It looked as if someone had deliberately put her into a pose that suggested an irritated or angry mood.

She didn't just fall to the ground in that position, Carly thought.

The second victim, Ariana Welch, had been found in the same public park. Her position was stranger and more artificial. She was on her left side, her legs parted as if she were striding along while her left arm trailed behind her. She seemed to be waving or pointing with her right arm. Odder still, her head and one arm and one leg were propped up on little mounds of something gray.

According to the descriptions, some sort of clay had been used to keep both of those bodies in a specific position.

Based on the scant information in front of her, Carly couldn't draw any solid conclusions about the killings, except that their ritualistic traits definitely suggested that they were, indeed, the work of a serial killer. And Carly could glean just one thing about his profile with some certainty.

He isn't finished. He'll kill again—and soon.

*

Lyle was waiting at the gate when Carly's flight arrived at the airport in Albuquerque. Her tall, lanky African American partner looked more concerned than happy to see her as they continued on their way through the airport. His furrowed brow and touch of gray in his hair contributed to his worried, fatherly appearance.

"How's that shoulder wound doing?" he asked.

Carly smiled a bit mischievously.

"What shoulder wound?" she said, rotating her shoulder, which actually hurt quite a lot. "Oh, *that* shoulder wound. I'd forgotten all about it. By the way, I had a nice flight, thanks so much for asking."

"I'm serious. I want to know. Because if you're not ready to get back on the job—"

"I'm ready, Lyle. I wouldn't have come if I wasn't ready."

Lyle growled under his breath and shook his head.

Carly started to worry.

It didn't bode especially well if her senior partner was having second thoughts about putting her back on the job. He could send her packing if he thought it was the right thing to do.

Lyle didn't say another word as they continued on their way outside to where a car supplied by the FBI Albuquerque field office awaited them. Lyle was still silent as they got into the car, and he started to drive.

"So, what can you tell me about the case?" Carly finally inquired.

"Did you get a look at the police files?"

"Yeah, on the plane."

"Then you know as much as I do, I guess. The weird thing is how the bodies were deliberately posed. We'll find out more at the new crime scene. We're supposed to meet the county sheriff there."

Another silence fell. Lyle's anxiety seemed more palpable by the moment to Carly.

Finally, she said, "I wish you'd stop worrying about me, Lyle."

Lyle shrugged as he drove.

"It isn't just the shoulder wound that's worrying me, kid. You went through a serious trauma very recently. A madman threw a knife at you. If he'd aimed better, or you hadn't dodged like you did, you might be …"

Lyle's voice faded, but Carly knew the words he couldn't bring himself to say aloud.

"You might be dead now."

Carly was well aware of that, of course. It was the closest she'd come to getting killed so far during her BAU career. But a little rest and a counseling session had really helped. She wasn't having nightmares, and she wasn't jumping out of her skin at every noise. She wasn't afraid of resuming work. In fact, she was more afraid of *not* returning to work. That's part of why she had insisted on coming here.

But Carly knew it wouldn't help for her to try to explain all that to Lyle, for one simple reason. Her brush with death had been more traumatic for him that it had been for her.

She knew that it brought up terrifying memories of how his previous young partner, Dawn Metcalf, had been killed in the line of duty. Lyle hadn't talked to her about it openly, and Carly only knew what she'd read in official reports about it. But she sensed that Lyle was still struggling with self-blame for his partner's death.

Worse, he was morbidly and sometimes irrationally afraid the same thing would happen to Carly. And there was really nothing she could say to make him feel differently.

Carly reached over and patted him on the shoulder.

"Lyle, you've just got to trust me. I know I'm ready to get back to work. I'm the best judge of that."

"OK, then. But I'm also kind of sorry about cutting short your visit with your folks."

Carly let out a chuckle.

"I'm glad you did. I'm not sure I could have stood another minute of it."

Lyle glanced over at her with surprise.

"That bad, huh?"

"Yeah, pretty much,"

"Do you want to talk about it?"

"Naw, not really."

"Are you sure? Because that's what partners are for. You know you can talk to me about anything."

Carly felt a twinge of discomfort.

Well, not exactly everything, she thought.

She'd never talked to Lyle about her mysterious ability, although she wondered if maybe he sometimes suspected it. But then, he never talked to her about the death of his partner.

Maybe it's OK if we keep a few things from each other, she thought. *That's worked well enough so far.*

"Maybe some other time," she said.

"Yeah, maybe."

They both fell quiet again, but this silence was easier than before. During their four years working together, Carly and Lyle had gotten to be perfectly comfortable not trying to make conversation all the time.

Besides, the New Mexico weather was a pleasant change. The temperature was mild, and the air was dry, and they were able to drive with their passenger windows open. And the rough, scrubby landscape was nice to look at.

Might as well feel like tourists while we can, Carly thought.

Pretty soon they'd be too consumed by the case to think about anything else but murder and mayhem.

As they drove into the town Teapa, Carly sensed from the modest but brightly painted homes and the bohemian dress of passersby that this was something of an artists' community. Soon they arrived at their destination—a public park with a gazebo a short distance away.

Everything there looked perfectly normal. Doubtless there had been reporters here earlier, but they seemed to have left the area. Lyle parked behind a police vehicle with a slouching man leaning against it. He was wearing a Stetson hat with a badge on it that clearly marked him as the county sheriff.

Carly felt a sense of relief as she and Lyle got out of the car and walked toward the sheriff.

We can get to work now.

CHAPTER SIX

As the sheriff approached, Carly saw that he had a frown on his face. She also noticed that he was chewing enthusiastically on something—either gum or tobacco—as he glanced back and forth between Lyle and her.

"You must be Sheriff Ketchum," Lyle said, shaking the stocky man's hand.

"And you must be Special Agent Lyle Ramsey," Sheriff Ketchum said, frowning up at Carly's taller partner.

Tobacco, Carly silently guessed, judging from the stains on his front teeth. That was a habit she hadn't seen for a good while.

Then, looking directly at Carly, Ketchum squinted with disapproval.

"I thought Pete Tully was going to be joining us," he said to Lyle.

Carly was sure she understood what the sheriff meant. This morning Lyle had told her over the phone that he'd been assigned an agent from the Albuquerque FBI field office. But Carly had taken his place.

"This is Special Agent Carly See, my regular partner," Lyle explained. "Believe me, she's the best there is."

Ketchum shook his head and spat a stream of brown liquid on the ground.

Definitely tobacco, Carly thought.

"I'm kind of used to working with Tully on cases like this," Ketchum said. "He's a good guy. But it's not my call, I guess. Far be it from me to complain."

Of course, it was clear that the sheriff *was* complaining in his own manner.

Is this guy going to make me out to be a problem? Carly wondered.

It wouldn't be the first time she'd inadvertently intruded on a "boys' club" of law enforcement. She'd learned early on to suppress her annoyance at having to overcome that sort of prejudice just to do her job.

Ketchum shrugged and said, "Well, I guess I'd better show you what it's all about. The second victim, Ariana Welch, was found over here just this morning."

As she and Lyle followed Ketchum a short distance along a pedestrian walkway, Carly gazed at their surroundings. Cottage Grove Park looked so tranquil that it was hard to believe that a murder victim had just been found here. Many of the pathways winding among planted beds and small green areas converged on a raised gazebo. People were strolling along, comfortably dressed for the rather hot day. Only a few gawked in the direction of the police tape that kept them away from the area where the victim had been found.

Ketchum lifted the yellow tape and led them toward a grassy area where there was a low fence. Pointing to a sign on the fence that said DON'T WALK ON THE GRASS, he commented with a sardonic grunt, "First of all, our killer doesn't pay attention to signs. That really gripes me, 'cause I'm a stickler for rules."

Carly and Lyle followed him as he stepped over the fence and walked across the smoothly cut lawn.

"Of course, the coroner's team took the body away hours ago. But I guess you've seen the crime scene photos, so you've already got an idea how the body looked. It was right here, in front of the flower bed."

From those pictures, Carly recognized the three gray mounds of clay on the ground that were still here.

"We've kept everything else the same," Ketchum said, pointing to the mounds. "She was propped up on these—her head resting on that one, her right arm on that, and her right leg on that. Lord only knows why."

Pointing again, he said, "The first victim was found over that way. She was propped up like that too, but not with as much clay. The pose was simpler. She was just lying on her back."

Carly crouched down beside one of the gray mounds.

"What kind of clay is this?" she asked.

Ketchum's eyebrows rose.

"Good question," he muttered, sounding a bit surprised that Carly was sharp enough to ask such a thing. "When you work around an artsy-type town like Teapa, you get to know about different types of clay. Truth is, you get to know more things about some of this stuff than you want to know."

In spite of his words, the sheriff looked a bit proud as he explained, "This is your ordinary modeling clay, not the kind for making pottery that gets fired in a kiln."

Ketchum scratched his chin and added, "The killer could be an artist, I suppose, but it's hard to be sure. I'm told there are different brands of this stuff, and I guess we might try to find where this originally came from. But that wouldn't narrow things down much because any kind of art supplies are easy to come by here in Teapa. We can do our best to trace it, but I doubt that we'll have much luck."

As Carly recalled the image of Ariana Welch's posed body lying in this spot with one arm flung forward, it was easy to imagine that the killer might be some sort of artist. But she knew better than to jump to any conclusions.

"How contaminated is the crime scene?" Lyle asked.

"Pretty badly," Sheriff Ketchum grunted. "Gawkers were already stomping all over here by the time the police arrived. It was the same at the first crime scene. There have been too many pairs of shoes all over here to get any useful footprints."

"Have you found any other material evidence?" Lyle asked.

"Nothing to speak of. There were no fingerprints at either crime scene, not even in the clay. Our forensic guys examined the first victim's clothing and didn't find any fibers or stray hairs. It'll probably be the same with this body."

Sheriff Ketchum shifted his weight.

"So you two are profilers. What kind of killer are we up against? More to the point, what should we expect next, and how soon?"

Lyle said, "The killer's probably male, and he's full of a lifetime of hate and resentment that's finally boiled over. And he's not finished killing yet, and he's probably going to only target women."

"So it seems we've got a lady-killer on our hands," the sheriff commented, looking dubiously at Carly.

She met his gaze evenly, well aware that with her average height and slender body, she was less robust than some female agents in the Bureau. But given room to move, Carly knew she was ordinarily quite agile and able to hold her own. Of course, that last conflict had caught her in an enclosed space, and right now she was at a disadvantage because of her wound. Even so, she had special skills that a man like this sheriff would never understand.

Lyle continued, "And my guess is, he's going to kill again soon. So we'd better work faster than he does."

Ketchum spat again.

"I was afraid you were going to say something like that."

Carly asked, "Do you have any suspects at all?"

"Not at this time," Ketchum said.

"Do you know where the actual abduction took place?" Lyle asked.

"Right outside the girl's house. She was about to go in when somebody jumped her. We know because we found her purse and cellphone where she dropped them."

"Tell me how the body was found," Lyle asked.

"Passersby didn't notice she was dead right away. A slew of dumbasses stood around thinking it was performance art. Lots of stupid stuff passes for art in a town like this, and everybody just nods their heads and gawks without paying any real attention. But the first person to point out she was *dead* is kind of an odd duck. His name is Toby Higgins. He's a local painter who was out walking his dog early in the morning."

"Do you think he might be a suspect?" Lyle asked.

"Well, I don't have any hard evidence for it. But he behaved kind of strangely when I paid him a visit a while ago. Doesn't like to answer questions. Kind of evasive. Surly, even."

"Where does this man live?" Carly asked

"Right near here," Ketchum said.

Lyle said, "We'd like to talk to him ourselves."

Ketchum shrugged.

"OK, then. Come with me, we can walk there in a jiffy.

As they followed Ketchum out of the park, Carly was glad to get a pedestrian's-eye view of the town of Teapa. She always found it useful to get a feel for the community where a particular crime had taken place.

She'd noticed during the drive into town that many of the residents had a distinctly bohemian look, and some of the older people looked like hippies who had become stuck in time. But now she saw that others identified themselves as tourists by the way they wielded their cellphones and snapped pictures.

Clearly people traveled to Teapa from far and wide to enjoy its charms and eccentricities. Businesses lining the streets included cafés, restaurants, art supply stores, and a range of gallerics.

Carly had taken art classes in college and was pretty much able to tell the genuine art from the kitsch. The grubbier, smaller galleries generally harbored the quality works, while larger, sleeker galleries tended to overflow with junkier stuff—the unoriginal southwestern landscapes, and the paintings mimicking Georgia O'Keefe with their outsized flowers and animal skulls. One seemed to specialize in replicas of much earlier Impressionist work—paintings of flowers, landscapes, ballet classes, and women in homespun activities.

Carly reminded herself of what Ketchum had just said.

"Lots of stupid stuff passes for art in a town like this."

Carly tended to agree, although she doubted that she and the sheriff shared the same idea of what was the "stupid stuff."

Meanwhile, Carly watched the passersby with the kind of wariness she always felt at this point in a murder case.

Any one of them might be the killer, she thought.

She wished her gift included the ability to detect a guilty person just by looking at them. Unfortunately, it didn't.

Soon Carly and Lyle followed Ketchum onto a residential side street lined with modest little bungalows.

They arrived at an attractive small house surrounded by a picket fence.

Ketchum unlatched the front gate and gestured to Carly.

"After you, ma'am," he said.

With a puzzled glance at him, Carly stepped through the gate.

She heard a deep growl and found herself facing bared teeth.

CHAPTER SEVEN

Carly backed up fast and pulled the gate shut again just in time to escape a set of snarling, snapping jaws filled with sharp teeth.

The dog that had growled at her looked like a German Shepherd. And it was definitely not friendly.

Sheriff Ketchum laughed.

"Oh, my goodness. I should have warned you about the nice doggie. So sorry to cause you such a fright."

Carly heard no note of apology in the man's voice. In fact, he'd set her up for a scare with his mock-gallant "after you, ma'am," inviting her to open the gate. He was obviously familiar with this dog's attitude toward visitors.

"Ketchum …," Lyle began, with a scowl on his face and the sound of a growl in his own voice. But the German Shepherd started barking loudly and any conversation was drowned out.

Carly was wondering how the three of them were going to make it across the yard when the front door of the house swung open. A tall, slender woman in a simple muslin dress stepped through the screen door out onto the porch.

"Jupiter, that's enough!" she shouted.

The dog ignored her. He kept jumping against the gate, barking and growling.

The woman loudly called out to Ketchum, "Sheriff, just go away. We've had enough bother for today. And Toby doesn't want to talk to any more reporters, if that's who you've got with you."

Ketchum called back to the woman, "Naw, these aren't reporters. These are FBI folks. They're here on business. They want to talk to your husband."

The woman stood with her arms folded, as if making up her mind whether to allow it. Then she stepped down off the porch, walked down the sidewalk toward them, grabbed the dog by the collar, and jerked him back.

"Jupiter, stop that!"

The dog obeyed with a startled, pathetic whine as she dragged him off the walkway onto the grass.

"Sit!"

The dog sat down obediently, but his ears were back, and he was fidgety.

The woman opened the gate and said, "OK, you can come in now. Jupiter gets to be a little overzealous when strangers come around. And we've seen more than our share of them today."

The dog stayed in place as Lyle stepped through the gate, followed by Carly and the sheriff.

As Carly eyed Jupiter uneasily, she wondered if she should release her weapon from her shoulder holster. Only the woman's "sit" command was keeping the dog from attacking them, and his obedience seemed conditional at best. She certainly didn't want to start out an investigation by shooting someone's dog.

But Jupiter managed to restrain himself as the group followed the woman to the porch. They passed through the screen door into a living room humbly furnished with what appeared to be secondhand furniture. Several large, lively, and colorful abstract canvasses hung on the wall.

"Let's see some badges," the woman said crossly to Carly and Lyle.

Carly was sure the woman didn't doubt the sheriff's assurance that she and Lyle were FBI agents. She just wasn't in the mood to make them feel welcome. Carly couldn't exactly blame her, after the kind of day she and her husband must have had so far.

Unless she's anxious for some reason, maybe even covering up for her husband in some way, Carly thought.

Carly and Lyle produced their badges and introduced themselves.

"I'm Dorothy, Toby's wife. And my husband and I will both be a lot happier if you keep your visit short."

She led the group through another door into a surprisingly spacious room that obviously served as an art studio. Carly could see that a wall had been removed to turn two smaller rooms into a single large one. There were dozens, maybe even hundreds, of large canvasses leaning against the wall and each other. They were in the same style as those hanging in the living room—abstract and cheerful, full of exuberant, swirling shapes and colors.

In the center of the room, a longhaired, bearded man about Carly's age stood working on another canvas. Carly was startled by how different this painting-in-progress looked from the others. The prominent colors were brown, gray, and black, and the shapes were jagged and unsettling.

Dorothy said to the artist, "Toby, a couple of FBI agents are here to ask you some questions—Agent Ramsey and Agent See, if I got their names right."

The man didn't say a word. He kept right on painting, peering at his work through thick-lensed glasses.

"Honey, did you hear me?" Dorothy said.

"Yeah, I heard you," Toby said with only the slightest glance at the visitors.

Carly remembered what Sheriff Ketchum had said about the painter a few minutes ago.

"Doesn't like to answer questions. Kind of evasive. Surly, even."

Was Toby Higgins a possible suspect?

Carly wasn't sure why, but she already had her doubts.

Lyle asked the painter, "Could you tell us about how you found the body?"

Toby still didn't glance away from his painting.

"He told the sheriff all about that already," his wife said. "Didn't the sheriff here tell you?"

Lyle turned toward Dorothy Higgins and said in a stern but polite tone, "Ma'am, I really need to get answers directly from your husband."

Dorothy shook her head with an irritable sigh and stalked out of the room.

Lyle stood waiting for Toby to say something. The man had yet to make eye contact with any of the three visitors. He was adding a series of ugly slashing strokes to his painting. He finally spoke in a low monotone, as if repeating something he'd already said over and over again.

"I was out walking Jupiter early this morning through Cottage Grove Park. I saw that a few people were staring at something on the grass. They thought it was a performance artist. But I thought …"

He paused for a moment.

"No, it was Jupiter who seemed to think something was wrong. He whined and got anxious. So, I followed him across the little fence and onto the grass. When I got close to her, I realized she was dead."

Sheriff Ketchum said with a skeptical growl, "How did you know she was dead?"

"You asked me that question when you were here before. It's like I said, I just knew. So did Jupiter, I think."

Toby sighed deeply and began to create an ominous gray shape with his brush.

"The police came, and I answered their questions. Then the sheriff came here, and I answered the same questions. Then the reporters came, and I told them I wouldn't answer any more questions, and to leave me alone. But now I'm answering questions all over again."

The man certainly sounded displeased to Carly.

But is "surly" the right word? she wondered.

She wasn't sure. And she didn't yet know whether this man might actually be the killer.

Carly asked the next question.

"Were you aware that there was a similar murder a couple of nights ago?"

"Yeah, I heard about it. But I don't know anything about it."

Carly wasn't surprised. She was sure the police had done their best to keep details about Gemma Gosnell's murder away from the public. Since the first victim's body had been found by a jogger in a more secluded part of the park than the second body, they'd probably succeeded reasonably well. But there was no way they'd been able to keep details of the second murder quiet, not with so many people at the crime scene.

"Did you know either of the victims?" Carly asked.

"I don't think so."

Sheriff Ketchum grunted, "What do you mean, you don't think so? Either you knew them, or you didn't."

Carly wished she could tell the sheriff to keep his mouth shut. If he'd just let her and Lyle ask the questions they might get more information. But she knew that Ketchum wouldn't respond well to any such suggestion.

Toby slashed a diagonal streak across the canvas.

"I didn't recognize either of their names. That doesn't mean I might not have run into them at one time or other."

"But you didn't recognize the second victim's face?" Ketchum asked.

"No, but …"

Toby fell silent and paused his work for a moment. Then he shuddered deeply.

"She just looked so … unnatural. If I'd ever seen that woman's face before, I'm sure she looked very different."

Ketchum scoffed aloud. But Carly felt less skeptical. The man's behavior actually didn't seem strange to her.

He suddenly stopped painting and turned his gaze on Carly.

"Can you tell me something?" he asked in a quietly desperate voice.

"I'll try," Carly said.

"Why … her?"

Sheriff Ketchum scoffed again and asked, "What do you mean, why her? You just said you didn't even know her."

Toby's expression darkened, and his voice became sullen—or *surly*—for the first time during their visit so far.

"What's that got to do with anything?" he snapped at the sheriff.

Sheriff Ketchum recoiled a bit, as if he'd just been barked at by a dog.

Toby added, "I can care about somebody I don't know, can't I? Well, I just want to know … why her?"

A silence fell in the room, and Carly knew there was no point in trying to answer his question. She understood exactly what he was trying to ask. She'd heard the same thing many times from people who had witnessed horrific crimes.

He wasn't asking some ordinary question about a killer's motive or purpose. He was struggling with a rush of irrational, guilty, and unanswerable questions.

"Why not me?" he was wondering.

"Why not my wife?"

"Why not someone I know?"

Though less well-understood than the "why me?" response to sudden misfortune, Carly knew that the "why *not* me?" response arose out of a spasm of guilt about escaping the same fate, of being a survivor instead of that other unlucky person.

Not everybody reacted this way. In Carly's experience, only people with a sufficient capacity for compassion did.

Toby resumed painting, striking more dark slashes onto his canvas.

Carly understood what he was doing. Until today, Toby Higgins's paintings had been free and lively, full of color and vitality and even humor. But a change was happening right before her eyes. Now the shapes and colors in his abstract compositions struck her as looking desperate, frightened, and hopeless.

I wonder if he even knows what's happening to him, she thought.

She exchanged a knowing glance with Lyle. From her mentor's grim expression, she realized that he'd come to similar conclusions about Toby.

Lyle asked the artist quietly, "Did anyone at the crime scene strike you as suspicious or out of place?"

“No, no one did,” Toby said in a numb, tired voice as he continued painting. “Yes, everyone did. I don’t know what to tell you. Everything and everybody seemed … all wrong.”

And they’re going to seem wrong for a long time, Carly thought.

She took a step toward him and said, “Mr. Higgins, I’m sorry about all you’ve gone through. I hope you don’t mind if I suggest that you seek out professional help. Counseling can really make a difference.”

“I’m fine,” Toby mumbled. “I don’t need any help.”

Lyle stepped toward Carly and gave her a touch on the shoulder that clearly said, *“There’s nothing more we can do here.”*

Carly more than agreed.

Lyle thanked Toby for his time, then turned and strode out of the studio, with Carly and the sheriff following behind. As they headed through the living room, Dorothy Higgins stood at the screen door glaring at them with her arms crossed, as if trying to decide whether to let Jupiter attack them on the way out of the house. But of course, the woman wanted to get rid of them.

She opened the screen door and called out, “Jupiter, sit.”

Again, the dog sat fidgeting and nervous as Carly and her two colleagues made their way through the yard and out the front gate. Once they were safely on the street again, Sheriff Ketchum spat on the sidewalk and grunted.

“I wonder if that guy’s our killer,” he said. “I didn’t before, but now I do. It’s a shame we can’t just bring him. But I guess we’ve got to get some hard evidence first, right? Shouldn’t be too hard to do.”

Lyle spoke a bit sharply, “He’s not our killer.”

Ketchum stared up at the taller agent with gaping disbelief.

“How can you be so sure? You saw the way he acted back there.”

“Yeah, we saw it,” Lyle said. “He’s not our killer.”

Carly was glad Lyle used the word “we,” because she felt exactly the same way about Toby Higgins. He wasn’t a murderer, just a distraught witness who was going to suffer from a terrible experience for a long time.

Ketchum scoffed, “Does this mean you’re not even going to follow up on him?”

“That’s right,” Lyle said.

“So what *are* we gonna do? What next?”

“We’ll want a look at the body of this morning’s victim,” Lyle said. “And the first body too, if that’s possible.”

*

A few minutes later, Lyle and Carly were driving a short distance behind the sheriff's vehicle, following him on the way to the county coroner's office. Carly was glad Lyle wanted to see the bodies, although she didn't want to mention why. Oftentimes she got a powerful communication from a victim when she was in the presence of a corpse.

She often wondered if Lyle had any idea about that happening. Was that maybe why he'd asked to see the bodies this time? If so, he wasn't saying anything about it. She wished she could clear the air with her longtime partner—could discuss her odd abilities with him—but she was always afraid that the truth would sound too bizarre. She didn't want to upset their excellent working relationship.

Soon Lyle followed the sheriff into a parking lot of a cluster of strip malls, where the county morgue happened to be located. The low building looked like little more than just another retail store.

Both vehicles parked, and Carl, Lyle, and the sheriff walked toward the building. They saw a white-clad, balding man leaning against a wall smoking a cigarette.

As they approached him, Sheriff Ketchum said, "Here's our man—Roger Poole, the county coroner."

Ketchum waved to the man and said, "Howdy, Roger."

"Howdy, Garth. You happened to catch me during my cigarette break."

Judging from the number of cigarette butts at his feet, Carly guessed that the coroner spent a lot of his time taking breaks.

Ketchum said to the coroner, "I brought two FBI folks along to look at a couple of your stiffs—Special Agent Lyle Ramsey and his partner, Carly."

Carly bristled a little at the introduction.

"His partner, Carly?"

I've got a last name. And I'm a special agent too.

Roger Poole looked Carly up and down, as if he were trying to decide whether she was attractive enough to bother leering at. Once again, Carly was uneasily aware of having intruded upon a local "boys' club."

Poole said to Ketchum, "You mean the two murder victims, I guess. Well, come on in and have a look."

Carly and Lyle followed the two men inside. The morgue itself struck Carly as small and not especially well-kept. A single corpse covered by a white sheet lay on the only table in the room.

"Here's the one from this morning," Poole said.

Carly wondered—was she going to get any impressions from this body? It generally helped for her to actually touch a corpse in order to make any connection with the victim. With the sheriff and the coroner watching her every move, was she going to get a chance to do that this time?

But she quickly found out that touching the corpse wasn't necessary.

As soon as Poole pulled the sheet back to reveal the victim's face, Carly felt a crushing force that almost knocked her off her feet.

I can't breathe, she realized.

CHAPTER EIGHT

A wild terror swept over Carly—the kind of terror she'd experienced a few times when a fall or a blow had knocked the wind out of her lungs, and she couldn't get it back again for several awful breathless moments.

Her mouth remained shut, and she couldn't catch even the tiniest intake of air. It was as if she been plunged into some sort of liquid that was much thicker than water—too thick even to force its way into her nostrils. The morgue began to swim around her and dissolve. For a moment everything went black.

Then she saw the face …

A woman's face gleamed brightly in the darkness, not more than a foot in front of her. The face seemed to be staring right into her eyes—but that was impossible. The face had no eyes, only empty gaping sockets.

Carly tried to cry out "Help me!" to the face, but she couldn't make a sound.

Suddenly air rushed into Carly's lungs again. Gasping, she opened her eyes and realized she was leaning with both hands on the edge of the stainless steel table with the dead woman on it.

She heard Coroner Poole let out a surprised chuckle.

"Hey, girl, don't throw up on the corpse."

Sheriff Ketchum chuckled as well and added, "You should have told us you've never seen a dead body before."

Grabbing Carly by the arm to try to support her, Lyle snapped at the two men, "She's seen plenty of corpses."

Grateful for Lyle's support, Carly pulled her hands away from the table and straightened herself upright.

Still holding her by the arm, Lyle gazed at her with a look that silently asked, *"Are you going to be OK?"*

"I'm fine," she murmured. "Let's get on with this."

Carly deliberately slowed her uneven breath, trying not to attract more attention than she had already. The room stopped spinning, and she was able to get a better look at the corpse on the table.

Now she was able to see the uncovered body, with the grotesque autopsy scars carved in a Y starting at the shoulders and continuing all the way down the abdomen. The enormous, untidy stitches looked fresh and new.

Her attention was especially drawn to the head and face. Certain details that she'd noticed in the crime scene photographs were markedly more noticeable now. Again, Carly observed that the victim's hairline had been shaved back so that the front half of her head was completely bald. But now she could see that the victim's eyebrows and even eyelashes had also been shaved away, and there was a peculiar paleness about all the features.

But what struck Carly most was that this was definitely not the face she'd glimpsed in her breathless vision. This was a lean face, and that eyeless visage had been wider, with larger features.

But why did I see it? Carly wondered.

She asked the coroner, "What can you tell me about the head and face?"

"Aside from how they were shaved, you mean? Well, they were scrubbed as clean as can be on both victims."

"What about the rest of the body?" Lyle asked.

"No evidence of the same kind of scrubbing elsewhere. Just the head and face. It's like maybe the killer was trying to get rid of any material evidence. Either that, or it's some kind of fetish."

Carly was open to either possibility.

Lyle put in, "I understand that the first victim died of suffocation."

"That's right. And now I've been able to determine that this one died the same way."

Lyle bent over for a closer look.

"I don't see any signs of bruising or a struggle. Even if she'd been smothered by a pillow, there ought to be some sign of that. What caused the suffocation?"

Poole shuddered a little and said, "I don't know for sure. All I know is that it was a pretty horrible ordeal. I got some blood work back for the first victim from our toxicology team. They found something in the first victim's bloodstream, and I'm pretty sure it'll be the same with this body here."

"What did they find?" Lyle asked.

"A substance called vecuronium, a drug used in general surgical anesthesia."

Poole pointed to a mark in the crook of the victim's right arm.

"You can see where it was administered intravenously. It's a neuromuscular blocking agent, a paralytic drug. It's used in really delicate surgeries where the slightest bodily movement, even a twitch, can cause dangerous consequences. Vecuronium completely immobilizes the whole body."

"Do you mean that she couldn't breathe?" Carly asked, remembering her own struggle for air.

"I doubt that was the cause of the suffocation. A full clinical dosage would paralyze the respiratory system, requiring that the patient be intubated, hooked up to a breathing tube and a ventilator. But I don't think these women got a sufficient dosage for that. They got just enough to be physically paralyzed, completely immobile and helpless. The worst part of it was that the victims would have been fully conscious through whatever happened to them. It must have been an awful way to die."

Awful is right, Carly thought.

Carly understood now that the victim had been communicating to her the horrible sensations of suffocation.

"I also found traces of chloroform in both of their nasal passages," Poole said. "My guess is the killer used it as a knockout drug to abduct them."

But what about the eyeless face? she wondered. *Why did I see that?*

Ketchum asked, "What are the chances of us tracking down the sources of these two drugs?"

Poole shook his head.

"There's not much of a chance with the chloroform. It's easy to make out of readily available household ingredients—bleach and acetone, usually. Our killer probably mixed it up himself."

Lyle asked Coroner Poole, "Where might he have obtained the anesthetic?"

"From a hospital, most likely."

"So does that mean the killer is a surgeon?" Sheriff Ketchum asked. "Or maybe an anesthesiologist?"

"Not necessarily. All it means is that the killer managed to get his hands on some vecuronium. Maybe he stole it, pure and simple. Or paid someone else to steal it."

Ketchum put in, "So I guess we need to check with hospitals in the area to find out whether any of this drug has gone missing."

"You can try," Poole put in. "But a theft like that might have gone unnoticed."

Lyle asked Poole, "Have you still got Gemma Gosnell's body?"

Poole glanced at his watch.

"Yeah, and you got here just in time to have a quick look at it. The family's coming any minute now to claim it. Come on over here."

Poole led the group over to the wall with the cold lockers. He opened a drawer, and another body rolled out, this one not covered by anything at all. Carly's eyes widened at the sight of the victim's face.

This was the one she'd seen in her vision just now. It didn't have that same eerie gleam, and its eye sockets weren't gaping and empty. But the wider shape of the features was unmistakable.

Carly felt confused. It was clear that both of these women were killed the same way. Which one was trying to tell her that?

The coroner explained as he pointed out details, "You can see that her face was scrubbed clean, just like the other victim. And her head and eyebrows and eyelashes were shaved the same way."

Looking for an excuse to touch the body, Carly put her finger against the puncture wound in the crook of the victim's right arm.

She said to Poole, "And here is where the IV was inserted."

"That's right. She got the same dose of vecuronium as the second victim."

Carly touched the wound only for a second, so as not to draw attention to her action. Sometimes that was enough for a message to come through. But she wasn't getting any communication from Gemma Gosnell, at least not right now. That wasn't surprising, because this wasn't an easy process. Carly's gift seemed to wax and wane, kicking in at almost random moments.

"Have you got any questions?" Poole asked Carly and Lyle.

"I don't think so," Lyle said.

"Me neither," Carly said. "Thanks for your time."

"Glad to help. And I sure hope you catch whoever that did this. He's one mean bastard, I can tell you that. And I sure don't like the idea of him doing anything like this again."

Carly, Lyle, and the sheriff left the examination room and continued on out of the building. The second they set foot outside into the late afternoon sunlight, a black hearse pulled up and parked in front of the building. A smaller car parked right behind it.

Carly remembered what the coroner had said about Gemma Gosnell's body.

"The family's coming any minute now to claim it."

We really did get here just in time to see it, Carly realized.

A somber, dark-clad man stepped out of the chauffeur-driven

hearse—the mortician, Carly was sure. A couple of his assistants began to unload a gurney from the back of the hearse. A man and a woman got out of the vehicle parked behind the hearse and walked toward the front entrance. The woman was wearing sunglasses, and the man was supporting her by the arm.

Sheriff Ketchum introduced the couple to Carly and Lyle.

"Mr. and Mrs. Gosnell, these are Special Agents See and Ramsey of the FBI. They got here this afternoon. They're here to solve your daughter's murder."

Mrs. Gosnell glared at Carly and Lyle.

"You're a little late, aren't you?" she said. "Someone else is dead already."

Her husband said quietly, "Now Cody, try to be fair to these people."

Cody Gosnell let out a rumbling growl.

"Fair? I've got no cause to be fair. How fair is any of this to you or me? We've lost our baby, Walter. And now someone else has lost their baby as well. The FBI should have gotten here yesterday or the day before. The monster who did this to Gemma could have been stopped from doing it again."

Cody Gosnell turned her accusing gaze on Sheriff Ketchum.

"And if you'd been doing your job, none of this would have happened to begin with," she said to him.

Ketchum looked stung and shamed. Carly guessed that he wasn't used to dealing with families of murder victims. If he had, he'd have been prepared for this kind of outburst, unfair though it might be.

But Ketchum quickly recovered a semblance of his professional demeanor.

"The agents might have some questions for you," he said to the couple.

Cody's lips twisted into a sour grimace.

"Well, they can ask *you* for answers, Sheriff. You've already asked us every question anybody could think of. And we've told you everything we know."

As distraught as the woman was, Carly knew that she was telling the truth. The police records Carly had studied on the plane included a detailed account of Sheriff Ketchum's interview with the Gosnells. He'd actually done quite a competent job.

According to the transcript, Gemma had recently graduated from high school, but she'd still lived with her parents. While the young woman sometimes stayed out late, the Gosnells had become alarmed three mornings ago when she hadn't returned home after an entire night out.

They'd called the police and reported her missing, but of course Sheriff Ketchum hadn't suspected foul play at the time. The morning after that, Gemma's body had been found, oddly posed on a stream bank in the same public park where Ariana's body had been found this morning.

The truth was, Carly knew the couple really didn't know very much about what had happened to their daughter. Typically for a young person her age, Gemma had tended not to tell them very much about her activities or companions.

But Carly could think of one question the sheriff wouldn't have known to ask them a couple of days ago.

"Please bear with me for a moment," she said to the couple. "I need to know—did your daughter ever mention knowing a woman named Ariana Welch?"

"The girl who was killed last night, you mean?" Cody Gosnell said. "No, she never mentioned that name."

Her husband added, "That doesn't mean she didn't know her. If she did, we probably wouldn't have known about it. Now if you don't mind, we'd like to get her body out of this awful place. Could we do that, please?"

But there was another question Carly felt obliged to ask. It was a question that Sheriff Ketchum had dutifully asked them when he had interviewed them before. Carly wondered whether the couple had given it any further thought during the time since then. She actually suspected they might be rather obsessed with it.

"Mr. and Mrs. Gosnell, do you know of anybody who might have meant your daughter any harm?"

The mother shuddered at the familiar question, but she and her husband both paused and appeared to struggle with it anew.

"No. I can't think of anybody," the father finally said. "Everybody liked her."

The mother added, "Nobody could ever have meant our baby any harm—nobody except a monster."

Her eyes met Carly's.

"You've got to stop this from happening ever again," she said.

Carly shivered at the way the mother had singled her out for this command. Based on past experience with bereaved families, Carly knew that it was at least partly because she was a woman, and Mrs. Gosnell somehow expected her to have more compassion for her maternal anguish.

Then a sob escaped Cody Gosnell's throat, and she hastily turned away. Followed by the mortician and her husband, the mother rushed past Carly, Lyle, and Sheriff Ketchum into the building.

As Carly stared after her, she thought of the dead women she'd just seen—and especially of that weird, gleaming, eyeless face. They all seemed to be repeating the same words to Carly.

"You've got to stop this from happening ever again."

CHAPTER NINE

It's a monster, all right, Carly thought.

Cody Gosnell was right about that. A monster was loose in this apparently peaceful, artsy town where women had felt safe walking around alone at night. And she had every right to expect Carly and Lyle to do something about it.

Carly drew a deep sigh. Of course, they all intended to stop this killer before he struck again, but they had precious little to go on so far. And she knew that even once they did, the town of Teapa would never be the same. Certainly the lives of two victims' families were already changed forever.

She could tell by Sheriff Ketchum's pallor that the encounter with the Gosnells had hit him hard. He surely hadn't dealt with as many bereaved family members as Carly and Lyle had faced over the years.

Not that you ever get used to it, she reminded herself.

Becoming hardened to others' suffering would be a danger unto itself. But working with the BAU brought with it certain coping mechanisms, ways of not becoming desensitized to other people's emotions, but not getting overwhelmed by them either.

Finally, Lyle asked Sheriff Ketchum, "Did Ariana Welch have any family in Teapa?"

Ketchum shook his head.

"No, she'd recently moved here from Beloit, Wisconsin. She did have a roommate, though—Jolene Vaughn is her name. I interviewed her a few hours ago."

Carly exchanged a glance with Lyle. She knew they were thinking the same thing. A roommate might know more about the second victim's personal life than Gemma's parents had known about their daughter's.

"We'd like to talk to her again, if that's all right," Lyle said.

Ketchum scowled and put his hands in his pockets.

"Hardly much point in that, since I talked to her already. But I guess it's your call."

"You don't have to come along if you don't want to," Lyle said.

Ketchum looked at his watch.

"I'd just as soon not, if it's all the same to you. I've got other things to take care of, like checking out hospitals for missing paralytic drugs."

He took out a notepad and jotted something down, obviously relieved not to be having to deal so quickly with another distraught person.

"Here's the address where Ariana Welch lived. Do you want me to give you directions?"

"No, we'll use GPS to get there," Lyle said, taking the piece of paper from him.

"Suit yourself. Give me a ring if you need anything—or better yet, if you find out anything."

With that, Sheriff Ketchum headed back to his vehicle. Lyle chuckled a little as he and Carly walked toward their own car.

"I can't say I'm sorry he won't be joining us."

"Me neither," Carly said, remembering the sheriff's annoying behavior when they'd interviewed Toby Higgins a short time ago.

When they got into the car, Carly brought up GPS directions while her partner started to drive. With a frown creasing his forehead, Lyle seemed to be concentrating on the route.

Then he suddenly asked, "How are you feeling, kid?"

Carly was surprised by the question.

"I'm fine. Why wouldn't I be?"

Lyle grunted and said, "You didn't seem fine when we got our first look at Ariana Welch's body."

Carly winced as she remembered how powerfully her vision had affected her. She hadn't been able to breathe, and then she'd seen that eyeless face. Of course her leaning on the table and gasping for air had alarmed her partner. Even recalling that moment made her pulse beat faster.

"Yeah, I'm sorry about that," she said, as casually as she could manage.

"Don't be sorry. Look, after all you went through on our last case, nobody's going to hold it against you if you're not back on your game. Like I've been saying, you should take some more time off if you feel like you need it. The agent who was assigned to me from the Albuquerque field office is still available if you feel like changing your mind."

"I don't feel like changing my mind."

And she meant that more than she could say. The words *"You've got to stop this from happening ever again"* were still echoing through her thoughts.

"OK, then."

"But thanks for your concern."

"Hey, that's what partners are for."

As Carly continued to feed Lyle directions to their next destination, she wished she could simply tell him the truth about what had just happened. It seemed wrong to let him just keep worrying about her well-being, when she was actually feeling pretty good.

But how could she even try to explain this most recent episode? She didn't fully understand it herself—or at least not all of it. Of course, her terrifying spell of breathlessness had reflected the victims' experience of being suffocated.

But how *had* they been suffocated? Carly had no more of an idea of that than anybody else did, except that it had happened when they'd been helplessly paralyzed. She had felt the sheer terror of that.

And what about that gleaming face she'd seen? She now knew that it had been the face of the first victim, but why had it appeared to her in such a startling form?

Carly suppressed a sigh of frustration.

Always these riddles.

Only very rarely did she receive a full, coherent communication from the dead.

I guess it just doesn't work that way.

But she was grateful for even the smallest bits of information that she received. When the dead were trying to be helpful, they could support or direct her more ordinary tools of investigation. She pushed out of her mind those few occasions when the voices of the dead became more threatening.

Soon they arrived at the address they were looking for—a little wooden one-story house. A pickup truck with several boxes in the back was parked on the street in front of the house. As they pulled in behind it, a young man unloaded a large cardboard box from the truck and carried it toward the house.

As Carly and Lyle got out of their car, the young man stopped and looked at them.

"Can I help you with anything?" he asked.

Carly and Lyle produced their badges.

Lyle said, "We're Special Agents Ramsey and See, with the FBI. We're here to talk with Jolene Vaughn."

The man peered at them over the top of the box and shook his head doubtfully.

"I don't know about that. I'm Brian McPhee, her boyfriend, and I'm trying to take care of her. The sheriff was here earlier, and I think she's had enough talking to cops for one day. She's still awfully shaken up by what happened to Ariana last night. I think maybe you should wait until tomorrow."

Carly and Lyle exchanged a glance of irritation. She knew they were thinking the same thing. This guy was clearly taking charge of Jolene, and he expected to be the one making decisions here.

Lyle snapped at the young man, "I think we'll let her be the judge of that."

Carly followed as Lyle stepped past Brian onto the sidewalk that led to the house. As they stepped up onto the small front stoop, a young woman inside apparently heard their approach. She appeared in the doorway, but before Carly and Lyle could introduce themselves anew, Brian's voice called out from behind them.

"Sweetie, these folks are from the FBI. I tried to tell them you wouldn't want to talk to them, but—"

The young woman interrupted him, opening the screen door for Lyle and Carly. She was a small, sturdy-looking woman dressed in jeans and a multi-colored blouse. Her long brown hair was splashed here and there with streaks of blue.

"Come on in," she said. "I want to help however I can."

Carly and Lyle walked into the small, somewhat musty-smelling living room of what Carly guessed to be a cheap, furnished rental. The only bright spots in the room were some crystals hanging in a window, a little glass pyramid on a table, and a poster on the wall. The pyramid had what looked like a universe inside, and the poster showed a strong female face with a third eye in her forehead and stars circling her head.

Pretty New Agey, Carly realized. But she figured that wasn't unusual in this town.

Again, they took out their badges and introduced themselves.

"I'm Jolene Vaughn, Ariana's roommate," the young woman said.

Carly shook her hand.

"We're terribly sorry for what you're going through. And we know you've talked with the sheriff already. We'd just like to ask a few more questions.

"Sure," Jolene said with a welcoming gesture. "Please make yourselves comfortable."

At that moment, Brian came in behind them with his box still in his arms.

Jolene rolled her eyes.

"Brian, do you have to move all that stuff in here right now?"

"Don't worry, I've just got three more boxes."

He carried the box through another doorway into what appeared to be a bedroom. Without another word he left the house again.

As Carly and Lyle sat down on a threadbare couch, Jolene Vaughn plopped into an iron-framed sling chair. She shook her head and said, "He's just really worried about me, doesn't want me living here all by myself after what happened. He means well, but I wish he'd just ..."

Jolene's voice faded. Carly and Lyle exchanged looks again. Carly was sure they were thinking the same thing. On the same day that Jolene found out her roommate had been killed, her boyfriend seemed to be moving all his worldly stuff over here. It looked like something he might have already had in mind.

But what mattered most to the investigation at the moment was how much of a distraction he was going to be right now. Carly could see that Jolene was feeling tense and guarded.

Lyle smiled ever so slightly at Carly. The lines at the corner of one eye crinkled as he almost—but not quite—winked.

She managed to suppress a smile of her own. Although Lyle never exhibited any supernatural abilities, he did have peculiar skills of his own. And they weren't the sort of skills one got taught at the academy in Quantico.

"He's a good guy, isn't he?" Lyle said to Jolene in his calm deep voice.

Jolene stammered, "Yeah, he's—he's all right."

Carly didn't hear a lot of conviction in the young woman's voice. The situation in this house was coming clearer. It didn't take any supernatural messages to guess that Brian wasn't particularly concerned about Jolene's safety and peace of mind, if he was thinking about them at all. He was taking advantage of this awful tragedy to do something he'd probably wanted for a long time—move in with her.

Carly was sure that her partner had figured out all that and more, and he wasn't going to leave matters be.

Lyle leaned back and crossed his arms.

"Yeah, it's really important to have emotional support at a time like this. And I hope you don't mind my saying so, but I'm sure there are practical issues as well."

"What do you mean?" Jolene asked, crinkling her brow.

Lyle shrugged slightly and said in a perfectly pleasant tone, "Well, I remember what it's like being young and getting a start in life. Just paying the rent alone could be real tough. It's nice to have someone you can depend on to share all that."

He slowly turned his gaze to the poster that showed the strong-faced woman, but he said nothing more.

Jolene's eyes widened, and Carly suppressed another smile.

He's hit a nerve, she realized.

Jolene and her roommate had surely split the rent for this modest little place while Ariana had been alive. It would be nice if she could do the same with her boyfriend.

But she knows she can't count on him for that, Carly realized.

Actually, Carly guessed, he probably wasn't even reliable about paying the rent where he lived right now. He was taking advantage of this tragedy in more ways than one.

What a mooch, she thought.

And judging from Jolene's demeanor, she was thinking the same thing. Would the young woman who had just been hit with a tragedy be strong enough to stand up for herself?

Just then, Brian came in through the screen door with another box of belongings.

"Brian, stop," Jolene said. "Don't bring that stuff in here."

"Huh?" Brian said.

"I'm not ready for you to move in like this. I mean, I still don't know what I'm going to do with Ariana's stuff until her family comes to get it. Give me some time to myself, OK?"

"But don't you need me to—?"

"I'm fine, Brian."

After a moment's hesitation, she added, "Actually Betty Anne called me this morning and invited me to stay with them for a while. I'd like to do that."

"That bitch you work with?" Brian blurted, "But Sweetie—"

It was Lyle's turn to interrupt.

"I think she's made her decision, kid. How much of your stuff have you unloaded off that truck so far?"

"Just this box, and the box I brought in a minute ago."

"Let me give you a hand getting them out of here," Lyle said in a mock-polite tone. Standing up to his full height, he stared directly at Brian. Although Lyle was older, his athletic body and hardened expression made it clear he wasn't a man to be taken lightly.

Brian just stood at the doorway dumbly holding his box.

Lyle laughed slightly as he turned and walked into to bedroom. He emerged holding the box Brian had brought in before, then carried it through the living room and toward the front door. Brian hastily stood aside as Lyle strode past him toward the truck.

"Sweetie ...," he ventured.

But when Jolene just glared back silently, he slumped a bit then turned away with his own box.

Carly could tell by Jolene's expression that her self-control was about to break.

Sure enough, the young woman burst into tears.

"Oh, thank God he's gone. I thought I'd never get rid of him."

Carly took a package of tissues out of her pocket and offered Jolene one.

The roommate is ready to talk now, she thought gratefully.

CHAPTER TEN

Don't rush things, Carly told herself.

She sat quietly waiting for Jolene to regain her composure. Through the open front door, she could see Lyle and Brian rearranging boxes in the back of the pickup truck. She knew it would be just few moments before her partner finished disposing of the erstwhile boyfriend, but she thought Lyle would probably delay his return to the living room. He would give Carly a chance to talk woman-to-woman with the recent victim's roommate.

Gulping down one final sob, Jolene looked up at Carly.

"The terrible thing is, it was my idea for Ariana to move here to Teapa. We both grew up in Beloit, Wisconsin, and we were both unhappy there. The midwest just seemed so … boring. I got out and moved here and really loved it, and I talked her into moving too. I thought the spiritual vibes here were wonderful."

Jolene rolled her eyes and added, "How could I have been so wrong?"

Carly reached over and patted her on the knee.

"This isn't your fault. You've got to remember that."

"Oh, I know that. It's just so … sad, that's all. She'd been so happy in Teapa. All her life Ariana used to be all uptight and hung up, and she was really starting to find herself here. Why did this have to happen? I mean, what kind of karma could cause this? The universe plays terrible tricks on us sometimes."

"The universe," Carly thought, suppressing a sigh. While she'd never become involved with New Age ideas, she'd had her own experiences outside of ordinary reality. And sometimes her own wayward ability to connect with the dead seemed more like a cruel cosmic prank than a gift.

A sound from outside told her the truck engine was starting up. Then she heard the vehicle driving away.

We're rid of Brian, Carly thought, glancing out the screen door.

She saw Lyle stroll back to their own vehicle and get inside. As usual, her partner was being considerate, giving her time and space to talk to the victim's roommate alone.

Carly asked Jolene, "How did you find out about what happened to Ariana?"

Jolene fought down a stray sob.

"Oh, that was really awful. I'd spent the night with Brian. This morning a friend called Brian to tell him they'd found Ariana's body …"

Jolene shuddered deeply and continued, "And Brian told me. If only I hadn't stayed away last night. Maybe if I'd been here and she hadn't come home, I would have guessed …"

The young woman's voice faded.

"Jolene—" Carly began.

Jolene interrupted her with a nod and a slight wave of her hand.

"I know, I know. It wasn't my fault. It wouldn't have made any difference, would it? I just … wish I could make some sense of this."

I wish I could too, Carly thought.

"Did you know there was an earlier victim?" she asked Jolene

Jolene nodded.

"Yeah, I heard something after it happened. I didn't think anything about it. Ariana and I didn't even talk about it. Was it really the same killer?"

"We're certain of it. Did you happen to know the first victim? Her name was Gemma Gosnell."

Jolene shook her head.

"No, the name doesn't ring a bell. I don't think Ariana knew her either. She never mentioned her, anyway. Oh, by the way …"

Jolene reached for a piece of paper on the coffee table and handed it to Carly.

"This might be helpful. When the sheriff came by earlier, he asked me about the people Carly knew or hung out with. I was such a mess at the time, I could only think of three or four people. Since then, I've thought of some more."

Carly looked at the paper on which Jolene had written down a list of eight or nine names.

"Good thinking, thanks," Carly said.

Jolene shrugged and said, "I figured it was the least I could do."

Carly felt genuinely pleased as she looked over the list.

"Was she especially close to any of these people?" she asked Jolene. "I mean, was she spending a lot of time with any of them?"

"No. I'm pretty sure they were just casual acquaintances."

"Did she mention having any arguments with any of these people?"

"No. I mean, her life here seemed pretty conflict-free."

"So you don't think any of them might have meant Ariana any harm?"

Jolene scoffed slightly.

"I sure don't think so. Ariana pretty much got along with everybody."

Carly pocketed the list. She wished that all of her interviewees had Jolene's presence of mind.

She asked Jolene, "Do you have any idea of where Ariana might have gone last night?"

Jolene sighed and said, "I can only guess. I can think of a few places. She'd mentioned wanting to catch a new art exhibit at the Lacona gallery, and another one at the Birch Street gallery. She was also talking about taking a nighttime art class, but she didn't mention where and I don't know if it actually started yet. Oh, she sometimes liked to hang out at Jay's Café. Also at the Bighorn—that's a bar/restaurant."

Carly jotted down the information eagerly.

"Did she mention feeling threatened or stalked or anything like that recently?"

"No."

"What about you? Have you gotten a bad feeling lately, like you're being watched or followed?"

"I don't think so."

"What about anybody else you know? Especially women."

"I haven't heard anybody talk about anything like that."

"You've been very helpful," Carly said, rising from the couch. "Thank you for your time. And again, I'm very sorry for what you've gone through."

As Carly started to walk toward the front door, Jolene called after her.

"Agent See …"

Carly turned and saw that Jolene's expression had become more worried.

Jolene said, "Should I be … scared?"

Carly hesitated. She knew she should have expected Jolene to ask such a question. But how could she honestly answer?

Choosing her words carefully, Carly said, "You should be very *careful.* And you should encourage others to be careful—especially women. You said something about staying with a friend for a while."

"That's right. Betty Anne offered to let me stay at her place."

"That would be best, probably for both of you. It might be a good idea not to go out at nights, at least not by yourself. Stay inside. Stay safe until we catch whoever has been doing this."

"When will that be?"

For the first time during this interview, Carly was brought up short.

"Soon, I hope. I wish I could make any promises. I can't."

"I understand. Good luck."

As Carly walked out of the house, she noticed that it was getting dark quickly. Lyle was waiting for her behind the wheel of their vehicle.

"Thanks for giving me some space," Carly said, getting into the passenger's seat.

"I thought you might be able to use it. That boyfriend was one obnoxious kid."

"Do you think there's any chance … ?"

"That he's our killer? I doubt it. But I did put in a call to Sheriff Ketchum to have somebody keep an eye on him. What about you? Did you have any luck?"

Carly took the list out of her pocket and glanced over it.

"I've got some names, but I doubt that our killer is one of them. Jolene did mention a few locations where Ariana might have been last night."

"What do you think should be our next move?"

Carly thought for a moment. Then she took out her cellphone and brought up the police reports she'd perused earlier on the plane.

Skimming them over, she said, "At least we do know that Ariana was abducted right here, near her home."

"Because of her dropped purse and cellphone," Lyle agreed. "But we don't know where Gemma Gosnell was taken. Or even when."

"According to the report, she was apparently walking home from a movie. Maybe we should take a look at the neighborhood around the Gosnells' house. It's less than half a mile away."

"Maybe we should," Lyle said, starting the car engine. "Give me some directions."

As they drove, they noticed that the Gosnells' neighborhood was markedly less bohemian and more conventionally middle-class than much of the rest of the town. As night fell on the lighted streets, the area seemed almost eerily peaceful. Carly wondered whether life around here had ever been disrupted by a murder before.

They pulled up to the curb in front of the Gosnells' home, one in a row of modest, pleasant-looking two-story houses with small front porches.

"I don't see any security cameras on these porches," Lyle remarked.

"No, I haven't seen many in this whole neighborhood, and there weren't any near Ariana's house either." She referred to the report and added, "And the sheriff's team has checked for surveillance videos in the area. They didn't find anything useful."

Lyle scratched his chin.

"Our killer's probably smart enough to stay clear of neighborhoods with cameras."

Still reading, Carly remarked, "According to Sheriff Ketchum's interview with Gemma's parents, we know that she planned to go see some old foreign film at an arthouse theater called the Kasbah."

"So maybe she was coming home from the Kasbah when she got abducted. Let's see if we can retrace her route."

"OK. I'll give you her most likely route."

Lyle was following Carly's directions back into the more bohemian, artistic part of Teapa when something caught her eye.

"Pull over and park," she said. "We may have found something."

CHAPTER ELEVEN

The establishment Carly had spotted featured a big plastic sheep's head with enormous horns above the door. There was no sign bearing any business name, but she guessed it didn't need one. Judging from the customers cheerfully coming and going, it looked like the sort of place that all the locals knew about.

Carly's hopes rose as Lyle pulled into the parking lot beside the building.

She explained, "This must be the Bighorn. Jolene just mentioned it as one of the places where Ariana liked to hang out."

"That's interesting," Lyle said with interest as he turned off the car engine. "It seems to be directly on the route Gemma would most likely have walked from the Kasbah movie theater to her home."

Carly nodded and added, "Maybe the Bighorn is a hangout our two victims had in common."

The two agents got out of their car and walked through the brightly lit entrance. Inside they found a restaurant dominated by a bar with a couple of TV screens displaying sporting events. Booths lined two of the walls, and an array of tables filled the central area.

A tall hostess slinkily clad in a black dress with spaghetti shoulder straps glided up to Carly and Lyle.

"Are you looking for a table for two?" she asked with a broad, professional smile.

"Not exactly," Lyle replied as he and Carly both produced their badges.

"FBI?" the hostess inquired more softly.

Lyle nodded. "We're investigating the two murders that happened here in Teapa during the last few days."

The woman's eyes widened.

"Oh, I'm glad to hear it. Everybody's been scared stiff and on edge, especially since this morning when they found the other girl."

Carly glanced around the restaurant-bar. It didn't look to her as though everybody was "scared stiff and on edge." The mood at the Bighorn seemed relaxed and lively, with rock music playing. It seemed that a couple of murders weren't enough to dampen the town's bohemian party spirit.

Life goes on, Carly reminded herself.

Or maybe it was more like denial. In Carly's experience, some communities were slow to admit to their own horror over multiple homicides. Teapa could be one of those places.

Lyle asked the hostess, "Did you happen to know either of the victims?"

"I've heard people mention their names, but they didn't ring a bell. Of course, that doesn't mean they never came in here."

Lyle brought up a couple of photographs taken of both victims when they were still alive.

"Are either of these faces familiar?"

The hostess pointed to the photo of Gemma Gosnell and said, "This one, no. Not while I was on duty, anyhow."

Then she pointed to the photo of Ariana Welch and said, "But she's come in here from time to time, at least recently. My impression is she was new in town. So, she was one of the victims? Wow, and to think I almost kind of knew her. That gives me the shivers."

Carly asked, "Was she ever with friends? Or a date?"

The hostess shook her head.

"No, I'm pretty sure she always came here alone. She'd just head straight over to the bar and sometimes order something to eat right there. She seemed friendly—at least I'd see her talking to the other bar customers."

The hostess shrugged and added, "But I didn't have much contact with her. The person you need to talk to is our bartender, Molly Cross. She's working right now. I'll bet she can answer all your questions."

Carly thanked the hostess for the advice. Then she and Lyle made their way toward the bar, where a large, imposing woman wearing a white shirt and a narrow necktie was chatting amiably with her customers.

Carly and Lyle found a relatively unoccupied spot along the bar and tried to attract the bartender's attention discreetly.

"Are you Molly Cross?" Lyle asked when the bartender finally came toward them.

"That's me," the bartender said with a startlingly boisterous voice. "What can I do you for?"

Carly and Lyle produced their badges as inconspicuously as they could.

Lyle said, "We're Special Agents Ramsey and See with the FBI, and we'd like to talk to you about—"

Molly interrupted loudly, "Holy cow, the FBI! Wow, talk about your big guns! I hope you're here about the murders. The local cops aren't worth a damn, if you ask me. At least not about anything that serious."

Everybody at the bar and many of the customers eating at nearby tables turned to stare at them. Carly and Lyle exchanged a discouraged glance.

So much for not attracting attention, Carly thought.

So far during their day in Teapa, they'd succeeded in avoiding reporters. But the people who were starting to gather around them right now were likely to prove a similar nuisance.

"First things first," Molly said. "The two of you must have had a busy day. Have you had time to eat?"

Carly and Lyle looked at each other again. The truth was, Carly hadn't eaten anything since she'd had a snack on the plane this morning, and she knew that Lyle hadn't eaten all day either.

When neither of them actually answered, Molly said, "I guessed as much. Well, we need to do something about that." Slapping her hand against the bar, she bellowed, "It's not right for two law enforcement agents to have to do their jobs on empty stomachs. Are either of you vegan?"

Lyle and Carly shook their heads.

"That simplifies things considerably. You have to try our legendary 'hornburgers,' with all the toppings and our special secret barbeque sauce. They're the best burgers in Teapa."

One of the bar customers nodded and said, "They're the best in the whole southwest, if you ask me."

"How do you like your burgers done?" Molly asked Lyle and Carly.

"Medium," Carly and Lyle both said.

Molly flagged down a server and told him to get to the kitchen fast and order up two burgers. The man hurried away.

Meanwhile, other customers were still crowding around Carly and Lyle.

"So what's going on?" one of them asked. "Is there a serial killer in town?"

"Don't ask them that," another one criticized. "They're not allowed to answer questions like that."

"Have you got any suspects in custody?" asked another.

Carly stifled an anxious sigh.

We need to be the ones asking the questions, she thought.

Speaking over the rumble of queries from the people around her, Carly said, "Did any of you personally know Ariana Welch?"

A woman gasped.

"Ariana?" she cried out. "Was Ariana one of the victims?"

A man said, "Why, she was here just last night."

Another woman said, "Maybe she got killed after she left here!"

"Then it could have been any of us," the first one whispered loudly.

Carly's brain clicked away as she tried to decide how best to deal with the situation.

She said to the people gathered around them, "I'd like anybody who *didn't* know Ariana to give the rest of us some space to talk."

To Carly's relief, the group obediently started sorting itself out. Most of the people headed back to their tables, still glancing back at the agents and whispering to each other.

A few who apparently had some familiarity with Ariana stayed nearby.

As she got ready to talk with those who remained, Carly noticed that Lyle's attention was drawn elsewhere. She followed his gaze and saw that he was watching a man in a sports jacket sitting alone at one of the tables. The man's brooding stare shifted between his glass of beer and the activity at the bar.

Carly immediately understood Lyle's interest. That particular man seemed interested in them, but he was conspicuously staying away from them. In fact, he looked decidedly uneasy.

As Lyle stepped away from the bar and headed over toward the table, Carly thought about joining him, but quickly decided against it. If she did, everybody at the bar would follow her.

It's best for him to talk to the guy alone, she thought.

Meanwhile, Carly's task was to see if she could get any useful information from the people in her immediate vicinity. She turned to them and started asking questions.

*

As Lyle made his way toward the man who had caught his attention, he watched the guy's movements carefully. His body language was unlike anyone else's in the place.

Some Bighorn patrons were staring openly in the direction of the FBI agents. Others were ignoring them and concentrating on their own good times. This one was making a futile pretense not to notice that FBI agents were here asking questions. Between furtive glances their way, he stayed slouched over his table, staring at his own distorted reflection in his beer glass.

Maybe he's deciding whether he wants to talk to us, Lyle thought.

But then the man glanced across the room again, and he must have glimpsed Lyle's approach in the corner of his eye. He abruptly got up from his table, abandoned a mostly full glass of beer there, and tried to appear casual as he headed toward the front entrance.

If he had been trying to make up his mind whether to talk to the agents, he sure seemed to have decided against it.

Uh-oh, Lyle thought. *Something's up with that one.*

As he changed his own direction, Lyle looked toward Carly, who was still surrounded with people trying to answer her questions. He caught her eye, and with a silent tilt of his head indicated the departing man. Then he discreetly pointed toward the entrance.

Carly nodded and continued her questioning.

By the time Lyle made it out of the Bighorn, the man he was following had crossed the parking lot and was headed for the street. Then he glanced back and spotted Lyle.

Is this guy going to run? Lyle wondered. He didn't relish the idea of a chase that might well be futile.

But the man didn't quicken his pace at all as he started off along the sidewalk. Lyle moved a little faster until he easily caught up and walked alongside of him.

Showing his badge, Lyle said, "Sir, I'm Special Agent Lyle Ramsey, and I'd like to ask you some questions."

"Go ahead," the man snapped, still walking.

"Could we stop and talk for a moment?"

"We can talk and walk," the man said, glancing at his watch. "I've got somewhere I'm supposed to be. I'm running a little late."

O-oh-kay, Lyle thought. *If that's the way he's gonna be.*

This wasn't the ideal way to talk, but he could conduct an interview while in motion if necessary.

Falling into step beside him, Lyle asked, "What's your name, sir?"

"Larry Damon," the man said in an absent-sounding voice. Then he spelled out his last name: "That's D-A-M-O-N."

"Are you aware of the two recent murders here in Teapa?"

"Yeah. I've seen the news."

"Did you happen to know either of the two victims?"

"Not really."

"What do you mean, not really?"

"What was the first one's name again?"

"Gemma Gosnell."

"That's not familiar. I'm pretty sure I didn't know her."

Larry Damon's pace quickened a little, and Lyle walked faster to stay alongside of him.

"What about the other victim?" Lyle asked.

"Ariana Welch, you mean?"

Lyle's attention was piqued at how easily that name had popped out.

"Yeah, that was her name."

Larry Damon's pace suddenly slowed. Then he stopped walking and stood on the sidewalk with his hands in his pockets. Lyle stood still and waited for him to speak.

Without making eye contact, Damon said, "She was new in town. She'd lived in Beloit, Wisconsin, where she'd worked as a bank teller. She was looking for a change, so her best friend talked her into moving to Teapa."

Lyle squinted with interest.

"It sounds like you knew her pretty well."

Damon scoffed and shuffled his feet.

"I didn't know her at all. I just talked to her in the bar a little."

"When?"

"Last night."

Lyle felt small charge of excitement. But he knew that if this was the killer, drawing him out would still be a delicate process.

"What else did you talk about?"

"Nothing."

"Are you sure?"

"Yeah, I'm sure. I introduced myself and asked a few questions, and she told me a few things, but she really didn't want to talk to me."

He tried to hit on her, Lyle realized.

It was also clear that she'd rejected his advances. Had the consequences of her rejection been fatal?

"Then what happened?" he asked.

Damon fell silent for a moment. He gave Lyle a sideways glance.

"I sat by myself and watched her drink two or three Long Island Iced Teas while she talked with people at the bar—people she *wanted* to talk to. Those are really strong drinks, and I thought maybe she was getting a little tipsy. When she finally said goodbye to everybody and headed out of the Bighorn, I got a little worried about her walking at night by herself in her condition. So I went after her."

Damon grimaced slightly.

It struck Lyle as a guilty look.

Then Damon said, "When I caught up with her, she barely seemed to remember talking to me at all, so I tried to reintroduce myself, and I suggested maybe she shouldn't be out walking alone. I offered to walk her home."

"What did she say?"

"She said no, she'd be fine."

"But you didn't take no for an answer."

Larry Damon winced sharply. Lyle realized he'd definitely touched a nerve.

"I wasn't trying to be a pest. I just wanted to be helpful. But finally, she took out her cellphone and tapped in a number …"

The man let out a mortified sigh, then continued.

"But I could tell she wasn't really calling anybody. She was pretending to the call the police, to scare me into leaving her alone. It was really embarrassing. I just headed off in a different direction and wound up going back to the Bighorn, and I stayed there till it closed. You can ask Molly. She'll tell you that's where I was."

Larry Damon finally made eye contact with Lyle.

"I keep wondering if I was …," he began, but his voice choked and faded.

Lyle could guess at least some of what this guy was leaving unsaid. If he'd really been concerned about Ariana Welch, he could have been more insistent about walking her home. And if he had, maybe she'd be alive today.

And now Damon had to be wondering—had his creepy behavior been Ariana's last interaction with a human before she'd encountered her killer?

He feels worse than guilty, Lyle thought.

He feels ashamed.

Larry Damon shrugged and said, "That's about all I can tell you. I hope you can catch the bastard who killed her."

Then he walked away.

Lyle considered following him, but quickly thought better of it.

He's not the one we're looking for.

Lyle's gut told him so. And besides, the guy seemed to have at least a fairly good alibi—one that was easy enough to check up on.

Lyle watched Damon disappear around a corner, then he turned around and headed back toward the Bighorn.

He hoped that Carly was having better luck tracking the killer.

When Lyle walked back inside the Bighorn, he didn't see Carly anywhere at all. He'd hoped she was coming up with new answers from the customers who had crowded around her just a short while ago.

Did she just take off on her own again? he wondered. She was sometimes prone to do that.

For a few long moments Lyle felt a familiar panic rising. She was his junior partner, and it was up to him to watch out for her. Her recent wound would surely slow her down if she was confronted with physical danger.

But the words that resonated through his mind at that moment were not Carly's.

"Thanks, Lyle. You're always watching out for me."

He flashed back to the fierce gunfight that had taken his previous young partner's life—to the sight of Dawn Metcalf bleeding on the pavement, apparently unaware that she'd been fatally wounded.

Just before she died, she'd thanked him for watching out for her.

As soon as Lyle took another few steps forward, he spotted Carly sitting alone in a booth in the back. He breathed a sigh of relief. But he also realized that he was shaking. He was startled at how badly he'd overreacted to the thought that Carly might be in danger.

I'm way too easily triggered.

After all, he was her partner, not her nanny. And she was perfectly safe, sipping on a glass of sparkling water and poring over her notes so diligently that she hadn't noticed his return.

Glancing toward the bar where Molly was cheerfully serving customers, he felt a familiar insidious yearning.

Just one drink, he thought.

Just one shot of whiskey.

It wouldn't be enough to affect his thinking. And if he downed it quickly, Carly might not even notice …

Stop it! Lyle told himself sternly.

He'd struggled with sobriety ever since drinking had ended his marriage. Although he'd had an alcoholic relapse after Dawn's death, he'd worked hard since then to get sober again. Carly had never known him during his drinking days, and he wanted things to stay that way.

He steadied his nerves and walked to Carly's booth and slid into the seat facing her.

"How is it going?"

Seeming to notice him for the first time, Carly shook her head.

"I'm just spinning my wheels. Did Larry Damon tell you anything worthwhile?"

Lyle's eyes widened with surprise.

"You know his name?"

"Yeah, I asked about him after you followed him outside. Molly and a couple of customers knew him. They said he's a prominent local lawyer and pretty well off, and he kind of likes 'slumming it' around joints like this. He's sort of voyeuristic and doesn't interact with customers much, but he does hit on women from time to time. As far as anybody knows, he never has any luck. They all seem to think he's harmless."

Lyle chuckled. His partner seemed to have found out more about Larry Damon than Lyle had by actually talking to him.

Carly's good, he thought.

That was hardly news to him.

Carly continued, "Molly did tell me she saw him talking with Ariana Welch last night—hitting on her, probably. He even left right after she did, but he came back very quickly. Rejected again, she figured."

"Yeah, that pretty much confirms what he told me," Lyle nodded. "He must have been here in the Bighorn when Ariana was kidnapped. Did you find out anything?"

Carly shook her head.

"Like I said before, I'm spinning my wheels. About a half dozen people I talked to knew Ariana well enough to chat with her whenever she came in, but none of them knew her really well, and none of them knew anybody who might mean her any harm. And nobody seemed to have known the first victim, Gemma Gosnell. I guess we were wrong thinking she might have come here."

Scribbling on her notepad, she added, "Still, I can't help feeling like I should be able to connect a few dots …"

Carly was interrupted by a server bringing their meals. Lyle had completely forgotten that he and Carly had ordered hamburgers before he'd gone off in pursuit of Larry Damon. Now with the food in front of him, he realized how long it had been since he'd had anything to eat.

He eagerly took a bite, and the burger was delicious as promised. But Carly pushed her plate aside and kept drawing lines among the names and notes she'd jotted down.

"Carly, eat. We've both done all we can tonight."

"But Lyle—"

"I mean it, kid. You'll sleep better after a good meal. And we both need a good night's sleep if we hope to be functional tomorrow. It's liable to be a long, tough day."

Carly sighed and pushed her notes aside and began to nibble at her burger. But Lyle couldn't help worrying as they ate in silence. Should he have put his foot down about her coming back to work so soon after her trauma and injury? She'd had that strange spell upon seeing Ariana Welch's body, almost as if she'd been on the verge of fainting. Carly had never been the least bit squeamish about dead bodies before.

So what was that all about?

Like any other good law enforcement partners, Lyle and Carly had always been open and honest with each other …

Up to a point, Lyle thought.

He knew that his young partner was harboring some kind of secret from him. Would he ever find out what it was?

CHAPTER TWELVE

The man opened the door to the classroom in the Art Center building. To his dismay, he saw that the clay sculpture class was already underway. The nude female model had already assumed a pose on the well-lighted platform, and the other students were at their tables setting to work with their tools and their lumps of clay.

I'm late, he thought.

He hated being late. It meant drawing attention to himself, which was the last thing he wanted. But when he took a step backwards to leave unobtrusively, he heard a woman's voice behind him.

"Oops. I guess we're late."

He turned and saw a young blonde woman with short, spiky hair. He remembered that her name was Demi. As he stepped aside to let Demi walk on into the studio, he saw that the other students were looking at her rather than him.

It seemed like a lucky break. Maybe he could come on in without anyone really noticing.

Or maybe I should just leave anyhow, he thought.

The class wasn't proving to be all he'd hoped for, and he'd already been thinking about dropping it.

But before he could make up his mind, the woman who was teaching the class called out to him with a cheerful smile.

"Come on in. We're just getting started."

The man forced a smile and headed toward a vacant workspace. He figured maybe it was better this way after all. He didn't want to fall behind in his efforts.

He sat down and began to knead the clay with his fingers, but his eyes weren't really on the model. Instead, he was glancing among the female students who were working on their own lumps of clay.

He'd learned their names during the previous class, and the model's name as well, but he hadn't yet made a choice among them.

Which should it be? he wondered.

Layla and Margie were too dumpy for his purposes. Sierra had the right figure, but her face was far too unattractive, and Carrie was much too tall. Tia was too old, and Stephanie was too buxom, which left him with LuAnn or …

His thoughts were interrupted by a suspicious glance from LuAnn, who seemed to have noticed him looking at her. He abruptly shifted his gaze away from her and resumed shaping the clay.

Oh, well, she isn't right anyway, he thought.

And as for Demi, the woman who had come in late with him, her punkish demeanor wasn't at all what he was looking for. And he couldn't quite make up his mind about Vera, the model.

The teacher began to circulate among the students, examining each of their work as she spoke to the whole class.

"Remember, what you're making here isn't supposed to be permanent. You're working with non-hardening plasticine clay, not the kind you use for pottery and fire in a kiln. You'll learn how to make a mold from your completed clay figure, and then pour a casting mix into that mold to create your final product—a nice little sculpture that will dry rock-hard and look a lot like stone. You'll be pleased with the result, believe me."

The man almost laughed aloud. As far as he was concerned, not one of the dilettantes around him was working on anything with the potential of ever being pleasing. The sculptures they were going to wind up with would be dinky and ordinary at best.

Nothing like the masterpiece I'm working on, he thought.

He felt a twinge of awe as he visualized the epic bronze magnum opus he had in progress.

Then the teacher spoke to the model.

"Vera, are you comfortable holding that pose?"

The model shook her head and said, "It's getting a little tough."

"I thought so. Why don't you stand up and stretch for a moment, then take the pose again?"

The model stood up and smiled with relief.

"Thanks, that really helps," she said.

The man's mouth dropped open with astonishment at the change he saw.

His uncertainty about the model suddenly vanished.

What a transformation, he thought.

As she stood there naturally, the man now fully appreciated her looks. Vera was short but graceful, slim but shapely, and with her hair pulled properly back.

Perfect.

The model soon sat back down again, and he felt inspiration

welling up as he shaped the simple turn of her shoulders in his clay. He had to remind himself again not to give himself away with the quality of his work.

Don't let them see your genius.

Meanwhile, choosing his prey was always an enjoyable and challenging part of his process.

She'll do, he thought with satisfaction. *She'll do very well.*

CHAPTER THIRTEEN

Somebody's life depends on this, Carly told herself as she sat alone in her motel room.

Just a few minutes ago, Lyle had dropped her off here and told her, *"We both need a good night's sleep if we hope to be functional tomorrow."*

Then he'd gone on into his own neighboring room.

But Carly wasn't trying to sleep. She was trying to get a connection with a spirit that could help her prevent another murder. She wanted to spare another woman the horror of being suffocated while helpless but fully aware of what was happening.

She knew that her gift didn't usually work this way. Although she could receive messages from the dead, she seldom learned anything by reaching out to them. But neither the police nor she and Lyle had made any headway toward solving the case, either through conventional investigative methods or her own mysterious abilities.

Maybe, she thought, *some hint could point us in the right direction.*

She had to try.

There were a few techniques that had helped in the past. One of those was deep meditation, which she could use even in a setting like this. Her bland, characterless motel room was just like many others she'd stayed in when traveling with Lyle on FBI cases, with a threadbare carpet and furnishings attached to the wall or the floor. There was one difference. The framed picture on the wall was of a New Agey rainbow made out of children's glowing happy faces all braided together. Unfortunately, the image was too frivolous to help her reach the depth she needed.

She sat on her bed in the lotus position, feet tucked upon her knees. Bit by bit, she relaxed her body and her mind, feeling herself sinking into a pleasant darkness. As she slowed her breathing and counted slowly from 10 to 1, she felt as though she were drifting downward. She repeated the techniques she had learned and felt herself sink deeper, farther away from the familiar world. Finally, she began to see a faint blue glow that signaled she had reached a different state of consciousness—the deep state that would allow her to reach beyond the physical.

Visualize, she whispered to herself.

And for a moment, an image she was hoping to see floated back into her mind's eye. It was Gemma Gosnell's face, the same one she'd glimpsed in her vision when she'd been in the morgue earlier that day. Once again, the gleaming face was eyeless.

Talk to me, Gemma, Carly said in her mind.

But the lips didn't move. The image looked frozen and dead. Instead, an angry whisper came from a different direction.

"You have no right to be here."

Then she heard another and then another of the bitter voices. They sounded faint and far away, but she knew that if they drew near, she would begin to feel the threatening touch of dead fingers.

Carly pushed back, imagining a wave of pure blue light rolling over those spirits, washing them away. To her relief, they disappeared, but then the silent eyeless face she had summoned vanished too,

Carly found herself staring lamely at the back of her own eyelids. She was back to normal consciousness.

I've got nothing, she thought with a discouraged sigh. She was aware that not all spirits of the dead were friendly or wanted to be helpful. Fortunately, she seldom had to face those who resented her presence, but she had met them before and thought they could be dangerous. This time she had stopped them fairly easily, but she'd gotten nothing at all from either of the two murder victims.

What's the point of even trying? she wondered.

All told, she had the comfortless feeling that she'd been here a hundred times before—in a room like this, after a failed effort—feeling the same despair and discouragement. Somehow, she'd always gotten through that. And no doubt she would get through it again. But what kind of effort was it going to take, for both herself and Lyle?

Carly certainly felt exhausted now. She got up and went into the bathroom and took a hot shower. She dried herself off and got into her pajamas and came back into the bedroom just in time to hear her phone ringing.

She was surprised to see who the call was from.

"Hi, Dad," she said when she took the call.

"Hi, Carly. How are you doing?"

Carly was struck almost speechless. As commonplace a question as it seemed, it wasn't the sort of thing Dad asked her, practically ever.

"Um, fine, I guess."

"You're in New Mexico, right?"

"That's right."

"How's the case going?"

Surely he's not really interested in that, she thought.

Dad must be calling her for some other reason. She felt a surge of alarm.

Is something wrong at home? she thought.

"It could be going better," Carly said.

"What's it all about?"

Carly felt truly baffled now. Not only was she not used to such questions from Dad, but she didn't know exactly how to answer this one.

What does he want me to tell him? she wondered.

What should *I tell him?*

"Uh, there have been a couple of murders," she said.

"Do you think you're dealing with a serial killer?"

"It looks like it."

"Well, good luck catching him. And stay safe."

"Thanks. I'll try to do that."

A silence fell between them. Carly was sure that Dad was trying to figure out how to say something important.

But what? she wondered.

Her imagination filled up with terrible things that might have happened.

Finally, Carly blurted out, "How's Mom?"

She heard Dad exhale sharply.

"I'm glad you asked. She's … she's good."

"I'm glad."

Carly could hear Dad's voice shaking now.

"Listen, I know I … wasn't very pleasant to you during your visit. I got especially harsh when you mentioned Megan last night, and I'm … I'm sorry."

Carly almost dropped the phone.

She couldn't remember the last time she'd heard her father apologize about anything.

"It's OK, Dad."

Dad sighed deeply before he spoke again.

"The thing is … I don't know what you and Mom talked about after I left the room, but I've noticed a real change in her today. She's happier. She seems hopeful. I don't know why. But I haven't seen her like that in a long time."

Carly's mouth dropped open. This was absolutely the last thing she expected Dad to say. Apparently now that Mom had some time to think about the possibility that Megan was alive, she was feeling more comfortable with their conversation.

"Dad, I don't know how to explain—"

"I don't expect you to explain anything. To be honest, I … I guess I'd rather you didn't try. I just wanted to let you know that your visit really gave your mother's spirits a lift."

"I'm glad," Carly said, even though she felt too confused to be truly glad.

Another silence fell between her and Dad.

Finally, Dad said, "Well, that's pretty much all I wanted to tell you. I hope you catch your killer soon. Like I said, stay safe. And … come back to see us before too long."

Carly felt a lump of emotion in her throat.

"I'll do that," she said.

She thought about telling her father she loved him, but she decided against it.

He really wouldn't know what to say.

Instead, the two of them simply said goodnight and ended the call.

Carly got into bed and lay there for a few long moments, wondering why Dad's phone call hadn't made her feel happier. Then she remembered something else Mom had said last night.

"If your sister is alive, it's up to you to find her."

She let out a long sigh of despair. Hadn't she long since exhausted every possibility of locating her sister?

And what if Megan doesn't want to be found?

As she felt herself slipping into an anxious sleep, Carly reminded herself that there was still a killer to catch. He was probably lurking somewhere quite nearby, and she hadn't been about to find him, either.

She was afraid he'd claim another victim soon.

CHAPTER FOURTEEN

"Stop him!" a woman's voice cried out.

Carly couldn't see through the pitch darkness that surrounded her.

"Stop who?" she replied.

"Stop him!" the voice repeated.

Carly took an unsteady, stumbling step into the darkness. She tried to feel her way with her hands, but she came into contact with nothing tangible.

"Where are you?" she called out. "Who are you? I want to help."

"Stop him!" the voice said yet again, sounding tearful and terrified.

Then Carly realized that she was dreaming—lucid dreaming, when a person becomes aware that they are dreaming then continues with the dream. It happened to Carly occasionally, and it when it did messages came through stronger.

One of the victims must be trying hard to contact me, *Carly realized. But she could still see nothing at all.*

She asked, "Are you Ariana? Or Gemma? Or ...?"

Carly shuddered at the possibility that the killer had already claimed a third victim, and that she was the one who was reaching out right now.

But she could see no one through this darkness.

"Talk to me, please," she said. "I can't help you if you don't talk to me."

Then her reaching fingers touched something. A face, she realized. It trembled under her touch, and she felt a tear trickle down its cheek.

"Soon it will be too late," the woman whispered.

In another instant the face became searing hot beneath her fingers, and Carly yanked away.

A spot of light began to glow through the darkness right in front of her. But as the light grew brighter, it wasn't a face that she saw.

It was just light. It was just heat.

"Where are you?" Carly shouted desperately "Tell me!" ...

A buzzing sound jerked Carly fully awake.

Shaking off the remnants of the lucid dream, she rolled over and picked her cellphone up from the nightstand. She wasn't surprised to see that it was still quite early, and that it was Lyle calling. It wasn't unusual for her partner to be up and working at such an hour.

I wonder if he has weird dreams, she thought.

"Rise and shine, kid," Lyle said when she took his call. "I'm expecting news from our forensics tech guy in Quantico, and I want you in on the call, so you need to come on over here. I'm ordering breakfast from the lobby. What do you want?"

"A muffin with sausage and egg, if they've got it," she said, trying to sound more awake than she felt. "And orange juice. And coffee."

"Coming right up," Lyle said, ending the call.

Carly let out a discouraged sigh as she sat up on the bed. Just a few minutes longer and she might have gotten a clear message in that lucid dream, might have at least found out who was trying to reach her.

Maybe if I could just go back to sleep ...

But she couldn't do that. Lyle wanted to get back to their investigation right now. Besides, she wouldn't be able to step back into the same place in the same dream or even reconnect with whoever was trying to reach her.

As she put on her clothes, the woman's voice kept echoing through her mind.

"Soon it will be too late."

Carly could only hope it wasn't too late already, and that the killer hadn't claimed yet another victim.

She stepped outside into the gray early morning light and saw that Lyle had left his room door cracked open, so she didn't have to knock. When she pushed it wider and walked into the room, he was sitting at a table staring at his laptop computer screen. The breakfast he'd ordered had already arrived, and he was munching on a muffin.

Glancing over at Carly, he said, "Grab something to eat and join me."

Carly closed the door, collected her own breakfast items, and sat down next to him. As she unwrapped her own muffin, she saw that he was looking at the crime scene photographs of the two victims as they'd each been found.

Lyle said, "I woke up early, thinking about these photos—the way the victims were *posed* and held in place by those mounds of clay. That's got to mean something, but we haven't really concentrated on it."

"So far we've been busy doing the usual follow-up questions with friends and family," Carly said.

"I've been racking my brain about that ever since I got up." Lyle pointed at the two images on his screen. "The first victim's pose doesn't look like much. She's just got her hands on her hips. That could just mean anger or indignation. But the second victim looks really odd. If you'd prop her upright, she'd be standing with one leg behind her, her body twisted around and one arm outstretched."

Carly nodded.

"The first people who saw her didn't even know she was dead right away. They thought it was some sort of performance art."

"And in a way, maybe that's what it really was—on the killer's part, not the victims. He's putting on a show for everybody. But what is he trying to say?"

Carly thought for a moment.

"If he's thinking of them as models, maybe we should be looking at art classes—the kind with live models. Maybe there's a connection there. The roommate told me that Ariana had talked about taking a nighttime art class, but Jolene didn't know what class it might have been or even whether Ariana had started taking it."

"Maybe Gemma was taking a class too." Lyle reached for his phone. "I'll give Sheriff Ketchum a call and get him to work on this."

Lyle tapped in a number and rolled his eyes as he listened.

"I'm getting his damn machine. He must still be asleep."

"You don't know that."

"I'd bet money on it."

Then Lyle growled into his phone, "Hey, Sheriff Ketchum, rise and shine. This is Lyle Ramsey, and my partner and I are already hard at work. We need you and your people to do something ASAP. We need to find out whether Ariana Welch and Gemma Gosnell were taking any art classes—especially any classes together. And while you're at it, put together a list of all the art classes in Teapa that use live models."

Carly's eyes widened as Lyle ended the call.

"*All* the art classes with live models? Isn't that kind of a tall order?"

Lyle drummed his fingers impatiently on the tabletop.

"Well, he and his cops might as well make themselves useful. So far, they haven't turned up a damn thing."

Then Lyle let out a groan of frustration.

"For that matter, neither have we. After all the leg work yesterday, we should have made some kind of progress."

He added with a growl, "I guess it must have come to your attention that I'm not in the best of moods this morning."

"I noticed."

At that moment Lyle's phone buzzed.

"That must be Zack Elsperger. I'll put him on speakerphone."

Carly was well acquainted with Zack. He was one of the BAU's brilliant forensic technicians, a typically nerdy I.T. guy with round, black-rimmed glasses. Although Zack was a bit socially challenged, Carly knew that he was a wizard at what he did.

Zack answered the phone in his unmistakable nasal voice.

"Hey, guys. How is beautiful sunny New Mexico treating you?"

"It sucks," Lyle said. "Nobody told us there wasn't a beach."

"Really? Bummer. I won't go there on my next vacation."

"I don't recommend it," Lyle quipped. "So what have you got for us?"

Zack chuckled and said, "I think I've got a live one. I've been sifting and combing through names of guys in Teapa who turn up in our files. And boy oh boy, I found one dude who really stands out."

"Tell us," Carly said eagerly.

"Well, he is one slippery devil, and he's gone by a bunch of different names. He seems to have originally been Perry Jordan, and he was a photographer for porn magazines in upstate New York. He also tried his hand at running a massage parlor, but he ran afoul of the local mob's prostitution racket. Apparently got in real trouble with them. So he skedaddled and changed his name."

Carly and Lyle exchanged looks of mounting interest.

"Tell us more," Lyle said.

"Next he went by the name of Hector Twain, and he worked in Cedar Rapids, Iowa, as a registered nurse. He got busted for using fraudulent credentials."

Carly could hear Zack's fingers rattling over a keyboard as he kept on talking.

"He moved on to Sausalito, where he went by the name of Justin Bench and worked as a classical music announcer. He had some kind of on-the-air nervous breakdown, and he left Sausalito in a hurry. His next stop was Teapa, and that's where he is now."

"So what's his current name?" Lyle asked.

"And what's he doing for a living?" Carly said.

"He's a Chi Kung instructor, and his name is Murray Fiore."

"Sounds colorful," Lyle said. "Has he done anything suspicious or illegal since he showed up in Teapa?"

"Well, he's not shown up on the police's radar, anyway. But it's not exactly like him to live a normal life. He sounds like the kind of guy you might be interested in checking out."

"I'll say," Lyle agreed. "Where can we find this character?"

Zack read an address, which Lyle wrote down.

"Great work, Zack," Lyle said.

"Thanks. Lemme know if you want me to do any more magic."

"We'll do that," Carly said.

They ended the call, and Carly and Lyle sat looking at each other.

Lyle said, "So we're talking about a Chi Kung instructor, eh? I studied a bit of that along with my martial arts training during my academy days."

"Me too," Carly said. "It's like meditating, only you're using your whole body to do it, with slow breathing and slow relaxed movements and ..."

Lyle and Carly said the next word in unison.

"Poses."

Lyle cracked his knuckles against the table and said, "We'd better pay this guy a visit."

CHAPTER FIFTEEN

Maybe we're going to get a real break, Carly thought as Lyle drove them through Teapa toward the Chi Kung instructor's house.

She and Lyle seemed to have reason to hope so. Based on Zack's account of their potential suspect's less-than-reputable life, the man who now called himself Murray Fiore had spent years running away from one thing or another.

Is this where the running stops? Carly wondered.

But as they wound their way to the edge of town, she had trouble keeping her mind on whatever might be coming up. She couldn't shake off the memory of that face she'd touched in her dream, the trickling tear, the searing heat in her fingers, and that pleading voice calling out in the darkness.

"Soon it will be too late."

Carly dearly hoped that it wasn't too late already. If they were actually closing in on the killer, other lives might be saved. But there was always another possibility that worried her.

What if we've got the wrong man?

If so, they were wasting time right now—time that they simply didn't have.

As they approached the address they were looking for, they reached a cluster of small adobe houses on the edge of town.

Although these homes were modest, they had a charming, authentic look about them that was largely missing from the newer buildings in the center of town. Most of Teapa ranged from cinderblock and stucco reproductions of Old West styles to wooden houses that could just as well be in Currie, Illinois.

This little community must have been here before most of Teapa was built. Its charm was heightened by a nice view of mountains in the distance, and Carly couldn't help but wonder how their wandering con man had managed to land here. His house was a rust-colored adobe box much like the others, and an early-morning Chi Kung class seemed to be going on in the yard.

Lyle parked the car near the house, and they watched the activity for a moment. About 15 men and women were moving slowly and in unison. Their bodies ranged from stout and overweight and sleek and dancer-like. But their movements were startlingly graceful and synchronized, and their faces glowed warmly in the early morning light.

"I remember learning this in Quantico," Lyle said.

"So do I," Carly said.

Indeed, she remembered her Chi Kung lessons fondly. They'd been a refreshing contrast to the FBI Academy's training in a hybrid of martial arts for combat and self-defense, including Krav Maga, Karate, and Tai Kwan Do. The gentle Chi Kung lessons had actually complemented those more aggressive martial disciplines, helping to maintain a steady calm even while carrying out much more violent movements.

They both got out of the car and stood watching the class unfold for a few moments, either unnoticed or ignored by its participants. For a moment, Carly thought she must be hearing recorded New Age music.

No, it's windchimes, she realized.

A white-clad male teacher stood in front of the group, his own body flowing gently as he purred out instructions. He kept repeating one word again and again.

"Chi rises … *chi* flows out … *chi* expands … *chi* falls … *chi* disperses …"

Carly remembered well the concept of *chi,* a word that literally meant "air" or "breath," the ever-flowing life force at the heart of Chinese philosophy and medicine.

She carefully observed the participants' movements. As the whole body swayed on slightly bent knees, the right arm circled out and then back across the abdomen, followed by the left arm circling out and back again, creating an elegant figure-eight pattern.

Carly thought back to the second murder victim's strange pose.

Is it anything like this? she wondered.

There was at least a slight resemblance to the leaning position and extended right arm of the second victim. But Carly cautioned herself not to jump to any conclusions. The killer had gone to some trouble to hold those bodies in exact positions, and she didn't see either of those reproduced here.

Meanwhile, the teacher kept giving instructions to the accompaniment of the tinkling windchimes.

"Strengthen your aura …Use flow rather than force … Bring chi up through the earth and down through the heavens … Don't disrupt the flow of chi with any tension …"

The instructor was a graceful, athletically built man with blond hair tied back in a ponytail. His jaw was strong, and his blue eyes radiated confidence and benign authority, and his expression seemed kindly, warm, and sincere. Carly wondered—could this possibly be the disreputable character Zack had described over the phone?

At the moment it seemed hard to believe. Still, it wasn't like Zack to make mistakes about this kind of thing.

Lyle gave Carly a nudge and said with a slight chuckle, "Think we might want to join in before we get down to business? I'll bet it would do us both some good."

Carly smiled and nudged him back.

"Sorry, but I think we'd better get to work."

"Yeah, I guess we don't want to get too mellowed out right now," Lyle said with a sigh. "We might have some ass to kick pretty soon."

Carly and Lyle walked toward the house until they came into full view of the instructor. Without pausing in his movements, he looked out at them with an inquisitive expression.

Lyle gave him a wave to indicate that he and Carly wanted to talk to him.

The instructor fell still, then said to the participant standing next to him, "Keep things going for a few moments."

The other participant nodded and started issuing the same sort of instructions while the teacher walked toward Carly and Lyle.

"What can I do for you?" he asked with a winning smile.

"Is your name Murray Fiore?" Lyle asked.

"It is."

Lyle and Carly both produced their badges discreetly and unobtrusively. They both knew there was no point in alarming everybody there.

Lyle said, "We're Special Agents Ramsey and See, with the FBI. We'd like to ask you a few questions."

The man's expression darkened a little.

"Can it wait another half hour or so, until my class is over?" he asked.

"I'm afraid not," Lyle said. "It's really a very urgent matter."

Murray Fiore thought silently for a moment.

Then he said, "OK, but not right here. I don't want to disrupt my class any more than is absolutely necessary. Come on inside the house."

Carly and Lyle followed Fiore as he opened the front door and walked inside, and Carly and Lyle went in behind him. They walked through a small cheerful kitchen that had obviously been kept up to date into a more spacious room filled with pyramids and flowing sculptures and other New Age decor. A large picture window filled the room with light.

As Fiore turned and smiled at them, he slipped one hand into an enormous decorative vase. Then he raised that hand.

He held a pistol, and it was pointed directly at Lyle and Carly.

CHAPTER SIXTEEN

Shock ran through Carly's system as she stared at the pistol leveled at them. She stopped herself from reaching into her jacket for her own Glock. Out of the corner of her eye she saw by Lyle's slight movement that he was reacting the same way.

It was too late.

Fiore's fast, smooth movement as they walked into sunlight gleaming through the picture window had caught them both by surprise.

"Put your hands up," he snapped.

Carly exchanged a glance with her partner, who looked as embarrassed as she felt about letting this happen. They both raised their hands.

But what now? she wondered.

Surely this man wasn't going to shoot them both here in his own house with his class doing peaceful exercises just outside.

Then she recognized the cylindrical black tube attached to the front of the small semiautomatic pistol. He was holding a Beretta with a silencer—a noise suppressor—attached to it.

Fiore kept his eyes and his gun trained on them as he moved past them and closed the door to the room. With two doors closed between them and the people outside, Fiore might well be able to shoot without attracting attention.

He could get away with it, she thought.

Of course, what to do with their bodies afterwards would be another issue.

Maybe he's already got a plan for that, Carly thought.

Carly momentarily pictured both their bodies found in odd poses in some nearby park, because now there seemed to be no doubt—this had to be the killer who had already murdered two women and left them that way.

Lyle's calm voice interrupted her thoughts.

"I think maybe there's been some misunderstanding."

"Oh, I think not. I know why you're here."

"We don't mean you any harm," Lyle insisted. "We just want to talk to you."

"Ha!" Fiore snorted, the gun trembling in his hand a little.

Lyle said, "Look, all this drama isn't good for anybody's *chi.* If you'll just let me reach for my badge so I can show you again—"

"Not a chance. I know phony badges when I see them."

Phony badges? Carly thought. *Why does he think that?*

"You're both armed, I take it," Fiore said. "One at a time, and very slowly, I want you to hand me your weapons, handle first."

The two FBI agents exchanged another look. Carly could tell from her partner's slight nod what he had in mind. She breathed slowly, readying herself for the next maneuver.

Lyle reached into his jacket and took out his Glock, holding the handle forward as he'd been ordered. As Fiore reached to take the weapon with his free hand, Carly went into action. Lunging forward, she seized him by the right arm. Their captor's Beretta went sliding across the floor and out of reach.

In another blink of an eye, the whole situation was completely reversed. Carly and Lyle both had their Glocks out and pointed at Fiore, who was standing there with his hands above his head.

"Like I said," Lyle said in a calm voice, "there's been a misunderstanding."

"Don't play games with me," Fiore said. "I know perfectly well the Pitbull sent you. He's been tracking me everywhere. And now you've got me nailed. Go ahead, take anything you want. I keep all my money in the kitchen. If you're going to kill me, get it done with. I'm tired of running."

Carly and Lyle glanced at each other again. She knew they were wondering the same thing.

Who's the Pitbull?

"Trust me, we're not here to kill you," Lyle said.

"Then like I said, take anything you want."

"We're not here to take anything, either," Lyle said. "Look, I think maybe I understand what you're thinking. My partner and I know a few things about you, like how you got into trouble with the mob in upstate New York because of your massage parlor. I take it Pitbull must be the name of the mobster who has it in for you. But he didn't send us. We never even heard of him before."

Fiore squinted warily and asked, "If he didn't send you, how do you know about what happened in upstate New York?"

Lyle shrugged slightly.

"Like I told you before, we're the FBI. It's our job to know this kind of stuff."

Carly added, "We also know you've been on the run for a few years, living under different names in Cedar Rapids and Sausalito and now here. But we don't care about any of that."

Carly sensed that the man's panic was ebbing somewhat.

"Then what?" he asked.

"We could all just sit down and talk," Lyle said. "I for one would like to get my *chi* more or less back in balance, because right now it's a mess. I'm sure that would be good for my partner—and for you too."

Lyle gestured to Carly and nodded at the Beretta on the floor. He held his gun steady on Fiore while she picked up the little pistol, flicked on the safety, and put it in her pocket. Then Lyle put his weapon back in his holster, and Carly followed suit with her own.

Fiore blinked hesitantly and indecisively.

"OK, let's all have a seat," Fiore said, indicating several chairs around the table.

Carly and Lyle sat down, and so did Fiore. But she could see that their captive was very tense.

She said to him in a soft, reassuring voice, "I'm going to reach for my cellphone, not my gun. I think we're done with guns for now."

"OK," Fiore said with a nod.

When Carly had her cellphone in her hand, she brought up a pair of images of Gemma's and Ariana's bodies. Then she pushed the cellphone across the table toward Fiore so he could see the photos clearly. She watched his reaction carefully.

Fiore's eyes widened and he recoiled sharply.

"Good God," he gasped. "Are those women … dead?"

Lyle nodded as he and Carly both continued to study Fiore's reactions.

Fiore stammered, "I—I'd heard about a murder a couple of days ago, and another one last night. Are those the … the victims?"

"Yes, and they had names," Lyle said. "Gemma Gosnell and Ariana Welch."

Fiore said, "But why—why do they *look* like that?"

"Look like what, Mr. Fiore?" Lyle asked.

"Why are they—*posed?*"

"That's a good question, Mr. Fiore," Lyle said.

Carly was pretty convinced that Fiore's horror at the sight of the photos was sincere.

But he might be an excellent actor, she reminded herself.

It would certainly be consistent with what they knew about the life he'd been living during the last few years.

Fiore shuddered and said, "What a sick thing to do. Why would anyone pose bodies like that?"

"We were hoping you could help us with that," Lyle said.

Fiore seemed genuinely baffled now.

"Do these poses mean anything to you?" Carly asked.

When Fiore just looked blank, she added, "Do you use poses like this in your practice?"

"No. We use movement. Graceful flowing movement."

"Don't you sometimes pause in a particular position?"

"Not like these." He indicated the photo of Gemma Gosnell with her hands on her hips. "This has nothing to do with Chi Kung. All I can say is it looks like some kind of really sick performance art …"

His voice faded. Then he nervously tapped his finger next to the cellphone.

"Wait a minute. I think maybe I know. I think I know who could have done this."

Carly kept her eye locked on his face. Was he just grasping at anything to lead them away?

Lyle said in a bland, calm voice, "Maybe you can tell us who you mean."

"There's a performance artist right here in town. He's out of his mind. He's really twisted. I've had my own problems with him. He came to my class one day, and we were in the middle of things. He kept babbling about his terrible life. He even pulled out a knife and threatened my students with it. We were all scared to death."

"Then what happened?" Carly asked.

"Then he suddenly put his knife away and was all smiles and good cheer. He'd just put on a performance, he told everybody. It was what he called a piece of 'guerrilla theater.' He's actually getting to be kind of a local celebrity for pulling the same kinds of stunts. People say he's innovative and daring and truly creative."

Fiore scoffed and added, "If you ask me, he's not an artist at all. He's out of his mind. A genuine menace, a ticking bomb. And I wouldn't put it past him to do something …"

He pointed to the pictures and said, "Something really horrible, like *that.*"

At that moment, Lyle's phone buzzed. Lyle took out his cellphone, and Carly saw that the call was from Sheriff Ketchum.

Although he didn't take the call, Lyle gave Carly a look that silently said, *"We'd better get back to him."*

"We aren't bringing any charges right now, Mr. Fiore," Carly said. "But we may have questions for you later. We want you to stay in the area until we solve this case."

"I'm not planning on going anywhere," Fiore said. "But I'm telling you right now, you'd better check out Shane Crawford. I'll bet anything he's the bastard who killed these two women."

"We'll keep that in mind, Mr. Fiore," Lyle said.

Fiore got up from the table and opened the room door. Then he looked at them and asked, "What about my gun? It's legal."

Carly took the Beretta out of her pocket and ejected the bullets.

"Don't go pointing that thing around," Lyle told him.

The two agents walked through the kitchen and out the front door, then made their way past the people still carrying out flowing movements in the yard. When they reached their car, they looked back and saw Fiore starting to lead his class again. Carly was startled by his seamless transformation back into a calm, centered, confident, and guru-like Chi Kung instructor. She could hardly believe that this was the same man who had just pulled a gun on them and had seemed so fearful for his life.

When they climbed back into the car, Lyle punched Sheriff Ketchum's number in his cellphone, putting the call on speakerphone.

"What have you got for us, Sheriff?" Lyle asked.

"Maybe something. I did a lot of digging and phone calling, and I found an art class that both Ariana Welch and Gemma Gosnell attended. I don't know whether they happened to attend it on the same nights, though. Does that sound like a meaningful connection to you?"

Lyle and Carly exchanged an eager glance.

"Maybe," Lyle said. "Do you have a list of other people in the class?"

"In a manner of speaking. It isn't like the teachers of these classes all keep great attendance records. But this one gave me a bunch of names."

Is it possible ... ? Carly wondered.

Lyle asked Ketchum the question that had occurred to her.

"Does that list of names include a guy named Shane Crawford?"

Carly's breath quickened when she heard the sheriff click his tongue.

"Huh. As a matter of fact, it does."

CHAPTER SEVENTEEN

Carly leaned closer to Lyle's cellphone, eager to hear every word that Sheriff Ketchum was saying.

"Shane Crawford?" Lyle repeated. "He was in art classes with both victims?"

"Right. According to this list, the guy was a model at least a couple of times for those classes and some others."

"A model?"

"'Figure drawing,' it says on this list here. And the other one was called 'Painting from the Live Model.'"

"Is his name familiar to you?" Lyle asked.

"It rings a bell. I believe we've gotten a few complaints about him, nothing serious enough to arrest him for. From what I recall, he seems to be kind of a public nuisance. Why do you want to know? Do you think he might be a suspect?"

Lyle made a small fist bump and silently mouthed the word "Yes!" to Carly. But he was careful not to display his excitement on the phone.

"It's too soon to say," Lyle said. "Could you give me a home address for this guy?"

"I'll see."

A few seconds later, the sheriff read an address to Carly and Lyle.

"Should I send a couple of my guys to pick him up?" Sheriff Ketchum added.

"Not yet," Lyle said. "Agent See and I want to pay him a visit first."

"Want me to come along?"

Carly saw Lyle wince a little. She understood why he wasn't enthusiastic about this idea. So far Ketchum hadn't shown a lot of skill in such situations.

"It depends," Lyle said. "Have you put together a complete list of all the art classes in Teapa, like I requested?"

Ketchum let out a grunt of annoyance.

"I've been working on that with a couple of my guys. But it's a tall order. I don't see how we can come up with an absolute complete list. There are dozens of classes in a town like this, and some of them only last a session or two."

"Just do the best you can," Lyle said. "We need all the information we can get."

Ketchum growled, "Why do I feel like you're trying to push me out of the loop?"

Maybe because we sort of are, Carly thought with a smile.

"I don't know where you'd get such an idea," Lyle said. "Whenever we've got something, you'll be the first to know."

"But—"

"We've got to get going," Lyle interrupted. "We'll be in touch soon."

Lyle ended the call. As he started the car, Carly brought up GPS directions for the address Ketchum had just given them.

Carly asked her partner, "Do you think Shane Crawford is our killer?"

"Maybe. Right now, it's the best lead we've got."

As Lyle drove, the things Murray Fiore had said about Shane Crawford kept echoing through Carly's mind.

Carly asked Lyle, "Do you think maybe Murray Fiore was making that stuff up about Shane Crawford? I mean, about him pulling a knife in Fiore's class?"

"Why do you think he'd do that?"

"Well, to distract us away from himself, maybe."

"So you still think Murray Fiore might be our killer?"

"What do *you* think?"

Lyle chuckled as he drove.

"Well, he's a real character, I'll give him that. He's sly and smart, and he's able to change personalities at the drop of a hat. He's also definitely paranoid, and a bit out of touch with reality. I doubt very much that some mobster has been hounding him for years because he opened a massage parlor in upstate New York. He'd hardly be worth the trouble of putting out a hit on. I wouldn't even be surprised if 'Pitbull' was pretty much a figment of his imagination."

Lyle shrugged and added, "So was he being completely honest about Shane Crawford? If there's some personal grudge, he might just be trying to make trouble for the guy. We'll just have to see."

Soon they pulled into a neighborhood much like the one where Toby Higgins and his wife lived. The streets were lined with modest little bungalows with small lawns and gardens.

But this time the house they were looking for definitely stood out from the others. It had an overgrown, weedy yard and was in bad need of a new coat of paint. No car was in the rough driveway, and only a few were parked on the street nearby.

Lyle pulled their car up to the curb, and they sat there for a moment looking over the rundown condition of the place. It was apparent that no one who lived there cared about appearances.

When they got out and approached the front door, they saw that the doorbell was marked "broken." That seemed to Carly to be in keeping with the general appearance of the place.

Lyle knocked on the front door.

There was no reply.

He knocked again, louder this time. There was still no sound from inside the house.

"Not at home, I guess" Carly said.

"Maybe," Lyle said.

He knocked again, and this time they heard a hoarse woman's voice from inside.

"Who is it?"

Lyle called back, "We're from the FBI, ma'am. We're here to talk to Shane Crawford. Is this where he lives?"

"Yeah, but he don't have any business with the FBI," the woman said.

"We'd like to talk to him anyway," Lyle said.

"Not at home," the woman said.

"Could we come inside, please?" Carly asked.

Lyle and Carly exchanged uneasy glances in the silence that followed. She wondered if she should be checking around the building to be sure that Crawford wasn't sneaking out of the back of the house at that very moment. Then the woman's voice called to them again.

"Just be off on your way," she said gruffly. "I've got no business with you either,"

"We'd really like to talk with you," Carly replied. "It will just take a few moments of your time, and then we'll leave."

Carly heard a discontented growl from the other side of the door. It was followed by the sound of a chain latch and a lock turning. The door opened, and Carly and Lyle found themselves facing a small, wizened woman wearing an old, tattered housecoat and a pair of shabby slippers.

A cigarette was dangling out of the corner of her mouth. She smelled strongly of alcohol, and her eyes seemed to be out of focus. An old television set was on, but the sound was turned off.

The two agents produced their badges and introduced themselves.

Lyle asked, "Are you related to Shane Crawford, ma'am?"

The woman finally looked toward them as she replied, "I'm his mother. 'Mrs. Crawford' to you. What do you want with Shane?"

"Do you know where he is right now?" Lyle asked.

"No idea."

"Do you know when he'll be back?" Carly asked.

"I've got no idea about that either."

"Do you know how we can get in touch with him?" Carly asked.

"Huh-uh," the woman said with a shake of her head.

"May we come in?" Lyle asked.

"I just opened the door for you, didn't I?" Mrs. Crawford grumbled. "Come on in but keep your stay short. I've got a lot of stuff to finish up."

Carly got the distinct impression that the woman wasn't actually doing much except drinking and smoking. The small house was a mess, with dust and cobwebs and clutter everywhere. The window shades were all down, and a small table lamp provided a weak light. The place reeked of dust and cigarette smoke.

As they stepped inside, Carly glanced around. She could see through the kitchen to a back door with multiple locks. Anybody making a hasty exit through there would likely have made some noise.

The woman sat down in an overstuffed chair, apparently indifferent to the two agents' presence. Her fingers picked at a chair seam that was coming open, and her eyes turned to the silent television. There was a half-full bottle of whiskey on the table beside her chair. Mrs. Crawford refilled a glass and took a large swallow.

"Are you alone here?" Lyle asked.

"Hah. Don't it look that way?"

"Mind if we have a look around while we talk?"

"As long as you don't touch anything."

Carly glanced into a short hallway and saw a couple of open doors, one to bathroom. The hallway door nearest the living room was closed.

As Carly stepped into the hallway, Mrs. Crawford snarled out a protest.

"You can't go in there."

Carly's curiosity was piqued. She hadn't planned to open that door, but she realized that Mrs. Crawford suddenly seemed a bit more alert than before.

"Why not?" Carly asked.

"Shane wouldn't like it."

Carly felt a tingle of rising interest. It seemed too bad that she and Lyle didn't have a search warrant. But they were a long way from having probable cause to get one.

Mrs. Crawford seemed to be trying to focus her eyes on Carly now.

"I mean it," she growled at Carly. "Don't go in there."

"I won't. Don't worry."

Mrs. Crawford's focus faded, and she took another gulp of whiskey and turned her attention back to the silent television.

Carly saw that Lyle had moved to the opposite side of the living room, behind Mrs. Crawford. He was standing next to an open rolltop desk with his hands firmly in his pockets, peering down at a clutter of papers. Carly knew that Lyle could view any papers that were in plain sight as long as he didn't shuffle through them.

He might find out something there, she thought.

Carly figured she should try to keep Mrs. Crawford's erratic attention away from whatever Lyle was doing. She sat down in a chair facing the woman and asked the first question in her mind.

"Mrs. Crawford, do you know anything about your son's whereabouts last night?"

"Why? Do you think Shane did something wrong?"

Carly didn't want to discuss the murders with Mrs. Crawford if she could avoid it. The woman was obviously easily confused, and it was best to keep her on a single topic.

Carly said, "I just want to know—was he home all last night, or did he go out at any time?"

"I wouldn't know."

"What about three nights ago?"

"Like I said, I wouldn't know."

Carly didn't get the feeling the woman was being evasive and covering for her son. She probably really didn't know. It seemed likely that Mrs. Crawford lived in such a deep alcoholic stupor that she was barely aware of what went on in her own house. Or at least she didn't remember much that happened from one day to the next.

Mrs. Crawford stared at the TV again. Carly glanced around the room and focused on a number of framed photographs hanging on the walls.

They appeared to have been taken over a period of quite a few years, and in all of them Mrs. Crawford appeared younger, happier, and healthier than she did now. Two children, a boy and a girl, were with her in many of the photos. The children strongly resembled each other and appeared to be the same age. The photos showed them at a range of ages from toddler to adolescence.

Carly was struck by something truly odd about the photos. In many of them, someone's face had either been torn or cut out. Carly found it easy to guess who the missing person might be.

She cautiously asked the woman, "Is there a … Mr. Crawford?"

"I wouldn't know," the woman said, still looking at the TV.

Carly squinted at her with surprise.

Did she even hear the question? Carly wondered.

She wondered if maybe the woman thought she was still asking about her son's whereabouts and activities.

She leaned toward the woman, whose focus seemed to be slipping again.

"Do you have a husband, Mrs. Crawford?"

"Not that I know of. Not for a long time, anyway. I used to. He's been gone for a long time. I wonder if he's still alive …"

The woman's voice faded for a moment.

Then she said, "Not that it matters much one way or the other."

Carly was unsettled by this answer—all the more so because it seemed perfectly sincere.

Carly pointed to the photo on the table next to her and asked, "Is the boy in this picture your son Shane?"

The woman glanced over at the photo and said with a nod, "Uh-huh."

"He's a good-looking boy."

"If you say so," Mrs. Crawford said, looking at the TV again.

Carly meant the compliment sincerely. The boy had a warm, kindly expression. So did the girl in the photo—a sort of glowing quality.

But it suddenly seemed as if the girl's face was glowing ever more vividly, as if caught in a beam of light. Carly reached over and touched the face in the picture. She felt an alarming charge, like an electric shock.

Carly closed her eyes and shivered from head to toe.

Keep control, she told herself.

Now was no time to get swept away in a paranormal experience. And yet a spirit seemed to be reaching out to her, to tell her something, and Carly couldn't very well ignore it, so somehow, she had to …

Her thoughts were interrupted by the woman's voice.

"I told you not to touch anything."

Carly drew her finger back, and the mysterious tingling suddenly vanished.

"Sorry. Who is the girl standing next to Shane?"

The woman glanced again at the photo and shuddered deeply.

"I don't remember," she murmured before turning her attention back to the TV.

Carly was even more startled than before. The girl in the photos certainly looked a lot like the boy beside her. She was likely to be Shane's sister and Mrs. Crawford's daughter, or a close cousin at the very least. And yet the woman hadn't sounded like she was lying when she'd said, *"I don't remember."*

She's worked hard not to remember that girl, Carly realized.

She thought that Mrs. Crawford must have worked awfully hard not to remember a lot of things, including her own husband, whose image had been eradicated from the family pictures. For years now, this woman had been repressing a whole lot of past experiences.

It's taken a lot of alcohol for her to do that, Carly thought.

Just then Lyle spoke up.

"Thank you for your time, Mrs. Crawford. We'll be on our way now."

Mrs. Crawford didn't speak or look away from the TV while Carly and Lyle made their way out the front door.

"Did you have any luck?" Carly asked as they headed toward the car.

"Yeah," Lyle said with a grin. "I know where we can find Shane Crawford."

CHAPTER EIGHTEEN

"EVERYTHING IS THEATER" Carly read on the cellphone that Lyle was holding up for her to see.

"Where did that come from?" she asked. "What does it mean?"

"Look at the rest of it," he told her, handing over his phone.

The image seemed to be of an advertising flyer. At the top was a photo of a young man, and beneath that an announcement read:

"EVERYTHING IS THEATER"
a lecture on Guerrilla Theater
by the esteemed performance artist Shane Crawford
at the Teapa Community Center

She remembered Lyle hovering over that rolltop desk.

"You snapped this picture when Mrs. Crawford wasn't looking," she said.

"And I didn't touch a thing." As he started up the car, Lyle added, "We need directions to the Teapa Community Center."

She found the address via GPS and told Lyle how to get there.

As he drove, Carly studied the young man in the photo. She saw that he bore an adult resemblance to the boy she'd seen in family pictures back at the Crawford home. Then she noticed the date and time of the lecture.

"We might get there just soon enough to catch the end of it," she said.

"But read on," Lyle replied.

Carly scrolled the image and found the rest of the flyer text.

Shane Crawford's weekly performance piece
will be presented immediately after the lecture
in the old Pastaworks building.

This week's event is entitled "Why Aren't You Dead?"

Carly's eyes widened with interest.

"That's some title."

"Isn't it, though? It's all starting to add up. I heard most of your little conversation with Mrs. Crawford. I saw the family pictures too. The husband was obviously torn out of all of them, I'd guess because he abandoned them. And the woman couldn't even bring herself to say her daughter's name. What do you suppose is the deal with her?"

"Something not at all pretty."

"For sure. Some bad stuff has happened in that house. It sounds like a classic background for a serial killer."

"It sure does. But we've still got to prove it,"

"Oh, we'll prove it, all right. We've just got to get a look inside that room Mrs. Crawford didn't want us to go into."

"We don't have probable cause to get a warrant."

Lyle chuckled, "Not yet, but it's not every day that a potential suspect goes public like this. We've just got to pay attention."

"You think he'll give himself away?"

"If he really gets into it. It could turn out to be a very revealing performance."

Carly hoped Lyle was right.

We've got to stop this guy before he kills again, she thought.

Their route took them back into the more bohemian, artistic part of Teapa, just a few blocks from the Bighorn. They parked near the community center, a brick building that looked like it had once been a small public school.

Inside the building, a sandwich board sign in the hallway bore an advertisement for the lecture. An arrow pointed to one of the former classrooms.

Peering through a glass pane in the classroom door, they saw a young man circulating among a small group of people sitting in a circle.

Carly checked her watch. "The lecture's going to be over any minute now. Should we wait here for Crawford to come out?"

Lyle chuckled slightly.

"Why? There's no admission charge, and it's open to the public. I'm anxious to hear what our guy has got to say."

With that, he opened the door and stepped inside, and Carly followed. It wasn't a large room, and their arrival didn't go unnoticed.

Shane Crawford paused in mid-sentence, looked at Carly and Lyle, then turned back toward his listeners and pointed to a quotation on the blackboard:

"I can take any empty space and call it a bare stage."

Resuming his lecture, Crawford said, "So the great director Peter Brook was right. A stage is any place you want to put on a play. A little light helps, but hey, you can do a play perfectly well in the dark. A parking lot can be a stage, or a restroom, or a barn, or a factory floor, or a jail, or a garage, or a classroom like the one we're in right now. What else have we learned today?"

A woman raised her hand and said, "Everybody's an actor."

Crawford nodded and said, "That's right. We're acting all the time, whether we realize it or not. We have no authentic selves. We're nothing but masks. This class is a performance. Right now, you're playing the parts of eager learners, and I'm playing the part of …"

He shrugged and said with a chuckle and a winning smile, "… of a really boring teacher."

The listeners laughed, and several said, "No, no, not at all."

He's really got them entranced, Carly thought.

She knew that this kind of charm and panache could make a very effective mass murderer.

"And what else have we learned today?" Crawford asked.

A man held up his hand and said, "Any group of people can be an audience."

"That's right," Crawford said with a nod. "Even unsuspecting people, people who have no idea they're witnessing a performance. Now *that's* when theater can get really exciting, because the line between what's real and what's not real, between spectator and performer can disappear completely. That's what we mean when we talk about 'guerrilla theater.'"

Lyle gave Carly a nudge and whispered in her ear, "What a load of crap."

Crawford turned toward them, his smile widening. Carly wondered whether he'd actually heard Lyle's comment.

"For example," Crawford said "what about these visitors? What parts are they playing in this little drama of ours? Why do you suppose they arrived so late? Who do you think they are?"

He took a step toward Lyle and Carly and said, "Would you be so kind as to introduce yourselves?"

Lyle crossed his arms and said, "We'll wait till you're through."

"Oh, no, that wouldn't be right. You're part of the performance now. You might as well be public about it. It's only fair. These people have a right to know all about you."

"We'll wait," Lyle repeated.

Crawford stared at Lyle for a moment, then at Carly. Then his smile turned a shade more sinister.

"Ohhh," he said, wagging his finger at Carly and Lyle. "You're those two FBI agents, aren't you? Yeah, I heard that a couple of agents were in town investigating—what was it again? Recent murders."

He rubbed his hands gleefully as he turned back to the class.

"Well, our very own drama certainly has taken a remarkable turn. Suddenly we're in the middle of a play by Agatha Christie. It appears that someone in this room is a murder suspect. But who might that be?"

Carly saw that the group didn't seem to share Crawford's delight at this development. They were staring with wide-eyed alarm.

Pointing to individual participants, Crawford said, "Well, who *is* it? Is it you? Or you? Or you? Or you? It's useless to try to hide. 'Murder will out,' as they say. The killer must be brought to justice."

Then Crawford's mouth opened with mock surprise.

"Wait a minute," he said to the agents. "Surely you don't suspect … me?"

Smiling again, he held out his hands and said, "Well, are you going to arrest me or not? Where are the handcuffs?"

Lyle glowered at him silently, and Carly knew her partner wasn't going to give him the satisfaction of any response.

Crawford leaned toward Lyle, peering into his eyes as if daring him to blink while speaking in an ominous tone.

"You don't have any proof, do you? No evidence at all. And I very much doubt that you ever will. Still, I can't help but wish you good luck—or 'break a leg,' as we say in the theater."

Then Crawford glanced up at the clock on the wall.

"But look at the time! This brings my lecture to a most interesting and unexpected close. I'd like to thank our FBI visitors for adding a touch of mystery to our proceedings."

Crawford clapped lightly, and a few of his students followed suit somewhat reluctantly. They seemed quite startled by this turn of events.

Then the students got up from their chairs and filed out of the room, chatting with each other and making furtive glances in the direction of the two agents.

Crawford said to Lyle and Carly, "So are you ready to introduce yourselves?"

Lyle let out a grunt of dismay and produced his badge. As she got out her own badge, Carly sensed that Lyle didn't like the way Crawford had gotten the best of them just now.

"You guessed right," Lyle said to Crawford. "I'm FBI Special Agent Ramsey, and this is my partner Special Agent See. And as a matter of fact, we *are* investigating the murders of Gemma Gosnell and Ariana Welch."

"Gemma and Ariana," Crawford said with a tilt of his head. "So, they had names, did they? That makes their murders seem much more real. So, tell me—am I a suspect?"

Lyle growled, "You're doing a lot to make yourself one. For now, let's just say you're a person of interest."

Crawford's smile positively glittered.

"A 'person of interest.' Oh, I do like that. I always strive to be as interesting as I can possibly be. And the fact that the two of you find me interesting is extremely flattering."

He chuckled and added, "I hope you'll join me for my upcoming performance piece. The title alone will intrigue you, I'm sure—'Why Aren't You Dead?' It starts in a few minutes, and it's just a short walk away."

With that, Crawford turned and left them standing alone in the classroom.

Lyle shook his head with dismay.

"I hate it when they taunt us. They just get so damn smug."

Carly patted him on the shoulder and said, "Don't let it get to you. You know better than I do, the taunters always trip themselves up sooner or later. So will this guy."

"*If* he's our killer."

Carly was startled. Just during the last few minutes, she'd become all but convinced that Shane Crawford must be the man they were looking for.

But what if he's not? she wondered.

Apparently, Lyle was worried about that possibility, which meant she should probably worry as well.

When Carly and Lyle left the building, they followed a group of people who had just attended the lecture and were obviously on their way to see the performance. Two or three of them had gathered around Shane, who was basking in the attention.

Another four people hung back from that group as they walked along. They were close enough for Carly and Lyle to hear what they were saying.

"That got weird," one of them remarked.

"Tell me about it," said another.

One turned around and then told the others, "Those FBI agents are right behind us."

Another scoffed and said, "Oh, those aren't really FBI agents. I'll bet Shane hired them to pretend to be FBI agents and mess with our heads."

Another shook her head and disagreed, "I'm not so sure about that."

The first one spoke up again, "Does anybody think maybe today's the day when Shane is going to do *it?"*

Carly was struck by the emphasis the guy put on the word *it.*

"Who knows?" another said.

Another asked, "What are you guys talking about?"

Another laughed and said, "You mean you hadn't heard? Shane says he's going to end one of these performances by committing suicide."

Carly and Lyle looked at each and murmured in unison.

"Suicide?"

CHAPTER NINETEEN

"A public suicide?" Carly whispered to Lyle. "Do you think it's possible? Right now?"

"I dunno," Lyle replied as he took out his cellphone. "But this guy likes to be unpredictable. We'd better be ready for just about anything."

As they moved along with various people headed from the community center, Lyle punched a number into his phone. Carly realized that they were on a street that they'd walked along before, where cafés and art galleries lined the sidewalk. This part of town was charming in a touristy manner, and it hardly seemed like a suitable setting for taking a life, not even one's own.

"Hello, Sheriff Ketchum?" Lyle said into the phone. "Agent Ramsey here. You and a couple of cops should join us at a building called 'Pastaworks.' I assume you know where that is. There'll be a kind of performance act going on inside, and we've had indications that it might mean trouble. You'll find Agent See and me in there."

Lyle fell silent as Ketchum apparently asked if an arrest was imminent.

"Maybe," Lyle replied. "It's the guy we talked about earlier—Shane Crawford. He's going to be doing his thing and he's sounding pretty erratic. Be ready to make an arrest. But don't jump the gun. We don't want to mess this up."

Lyle ended the call and pocketed his cellphone.

He shook his head and murmured to Carly, "I hope I didn't just make a big mistake. Ketchum can be a proverbial bull in the china shop."

"You made the right call. We're likely to need some backup."

Glancing at thc galleries as they walked by, Carly recognized one that seemed to specialize in reproductions of 19th and early 20th century works on which copyrights had long expired. Now there was an array of small bronze sculptures in the window.

She was sure that the cowboy on a bucking horse must be a copy of a work by the American artist Frederick Remington. She figured a group of human figures must be works by the French sculptor Auguste Rodin, since one of them was unmistakably his famous piece called

The Thinker. Several figures of women also seemed familiar, although she wasn't sure from where or when. Some of those appeared to be dancers.

She and Lyle passed by that window quickly and found themselves walking by a gallery of Native American crafts. Soon they reached their destination—a two-story, abandoned brick building on a busy street corner. The faded sign over the entrance still designated it as Pastaworks.

They followed others into a wide and completely barren ground floor of the empty building. The windows were covered with blinds, and an area in the center was lit by four spotlights hanging from metal stands. There were no seats, just a single stool in the lighted area, so the audience was either standing or sitting on the concrete floor.

Shane Crawford was already standing there in the light, watching with satisfaction as spectators came inside.

It seemed to Carly that a respectable-size audience was gathering. Apparently, the performer was rather popular.

Or maybe they're hoping to see him die, she reminded herself.

Finally, Sheriff Ketchum entered, accompanied by two uniformed officers. Not going to much trouble to look inconspicuous, they stood among the spectators with stern expressions and crossed arms.

Crawford took that as his cue to get things started.

He said to everybody, "Ah, I see that members of the local law enforcement community have decided to join us today. We've got FBI agents here as well. Is anybody else here in an official capacity? Someone from the CIA, maybe? Or the KGB? Or the National Endowment for the Arts?"

This quip got a good laugh from the audience. Carly glanced at Lyle and noticed that he was now scowling. He clearly didn't like Crawford's teasing manner. As for Carly herself, she couldn't help but be a bit fascinated by the performer. If he was really the killer, he was not like any she had met before.

One for the textbooks, maybe, she thought.

Crawford rubbed his hands together and spoke again.

"As usual, I need a volunteer from the audience."

A nervous tittering followed. Carly sensed that no one was anxious to assume the role. She guessed that Crawford's past volunteers hadn't enjoyed the experience.

"What, nobody?" Crawford said with exaggerated disappointment. "Now you've hurt my feelings! Well, I guess I'll just have to make the choice by myself."

His eyes roamed over the audience until they fell on Carly.

"And I choose FBI Special Agent See."

Patting on the stool, he said to Carly, "Step right up, have a seat right here."

Carly was stunned by the man's sheer audacity. Still, she couldn't help thinking that maybe this was an extraordinary opportunity, and that maybe she could use his self-confidence against him. But it wasn't a decision she could make entirely on her own.

She looked at Lyle and silently mouthed the words, "Should I?"

Looking startled himself by this new development, Lyle hesitated for a moment.

Then he nodded and mouthed the words, "Go ahead."

Feeling vulnerable and exposed, Carly stepped out of the audience and into the lighted area.

Crawford patted the stool and said to her, "Make yourself comfortable."

Carly sat on the stool but feeling comfortable was out of the question.

"So tell me, Special Agent See," Crawford said, "what brings you and your partner to Teapa, New Mexico?"

This might be a better opportunity than I'd supposed, Carly realized.

Right here and now, she could reach out to a fairly large number of people in search of information. And if Shane Crawford really was the killer, maybe somebody here knew something about it and would be willing to say so.

Better than a press conference, she thought.

At least she wouldn't have reporters asking her annoying and aggressive questions.

She turned her attention to the audience and said, "I suppose everybody here knows about the two murders that have taken place in Teapa during the last few days. If anybody here has any information that might help our investigation, please speak up. The local police and the FBI are anxious to apprehend the killer."

A stony silence fell as she waited for a reply.

"Or you can even contact us separately," Carly added.

Then Crawford said, "You already have a suspect, don't you?"

Carly turned, and her eyes met his. She gazed at him silently.

"Excuse me, I misspoke," Crawford said. "The proper term is a 'person of interest.' We've already chatted about that. And I strike you as very interesting, don't I?"

Carly still said nothing—not for lack of anything to say, but in hopes of throwing him off his guard. He was clearly a man who was used to having things his own way. Carly had no intention of giving him that luxury.

She held his gaze for a long, uncomfortable moment.

He was the first to turn his eyes away. Then he began to walk around the stool where Carly was sitting.

"Let's get down to the theme of today's performance, shall we?"

Looking at Carly again, he asked, "Why aren't you dead?"

Carly couldn't help chuckling at the brazenness of the question.

"Do you find it funny, Agent See?" Crawford said, still walking around the stool. "It's a serious question. After all, in your crime fighting career, you've surely cheated death more than once."

Carly took note of his stalking pace and posture, as if he were a carnivorous animal and she was his prey. The maneuver was clearly meant to give him a strategic advantage that probably usually worked against his subjects. But Carly had no intention of going along with it.

She got off the stool and began to mirror his movements.

"What about you, Shane? Why aren't *you* dead?"

Sure enough, he looked more than a little taken aback. And she could think of one sure way of really unnerving him.

Physical contact.

That's the one thing he's not ready for.

She reached out to touch his shoulder and said, "Well? Aren't you going to tell me?"

But the second her fingers made contact with his shoulder, a sharp shuddering sensation passed through her whole body. It was the same sort of charge she'd felt back at Crawford's home when she'd touched the girl's face in the picture.

I'm getting a communication, she realized with alarm.

And she was getting it right here in front of a large group of people.

CHAPTER TWENTY

Carly felt as though her legs were about to give out from under her.

Steady, she thought, determined not to collapse in a heap right on the concrete floor in front of Shane Crawford, his entire audience, and even Lyle and the Sheriff and a couple of local cops.

Somebody is reaching out to me from the other side, she realized.

Although she felt dizzy and her vision was blurred, she somehow managed to stay standing. Then she heard Shane's voice, reeking with smug relief.

"What's the matter, Agent See? Don't you feel well?"

"Oh, I feel fine," Carly replied as confidently as she could manage. "I feel just fine."

Hold on.

She didn't dare close her eyes in order to focus better. But this spirit was persistent, and the message was strong. The air around her was actually swimming with images that Carly knew no one else could see. She had to process them in mere split seconds, as fast as her brain could manage.

She first saw two almost fully-grown fetuses in a woman's womb. Then the image changed to two newborn babies in a hospital crib, one swaddled in pink and the other in blue.

A boy and a girl.

And Carly realized she'd seen those same two in family photos at the Crawford residence. She had felt an electric charge when she touched the girl's face in the picture frame—a portent of the barely controllable storm of impressions that swept over her right now.

She had asked Shane's inebriated mother, *"Who is the girl standing next to Shane?"*

And she remembered the woman's shuddering reply.

"I don't remember."

Of course Mrs. Crawford had remembered. Nevertheless, she had done everything she could to expunge her own daughter from her past.

But why?

Silently, she managed to ask the spirit presence:

"Who are you?"

And now she could hear a girl's voice calling out from the depths of her mind.

"Bonnie. My name was Bonnie."

And then Carly caught a horrifying glimpse of that girl as a teenager. The lower half of her face was covered by a surgical mask, and she had a belt around her neck.

She was hanging dead from a doorframe.

"Because of Daddy," Bonnie's spirit whispered as she faded away.

Carly took a long, slow breath as she focused her eyes on Shane again. He was visibly pleased by Carly's moment of apparent confusion.

But now she was going to use this episode against him.

She repeated what she'd asked just before being overcome by the message.

"Why aren't *you* dead?"

Shane frowned with dismay, aware that Carly was regaining her composure.

Stalking slowly around him, Carly said, "That question haunts you, doesn't it? 'Why aren't I dead?'"

She hesitated before she said the next fateful words.

"'Why am I still alive,' you ask yourself, 'when Bonnie is dead?'"

Shane's eyes widened, and he froze in place.

The audience fell completely silent.

"You think you *ought* to be dead, don't you?" Carly continued. "You think you deserve to be dead. You didn't defend Bonnie … when *Daddy* was doing terrible things to her. You didn't even try. And finally, Bonnie took her own life."

Shane was trembling now. Carly stepped closer to him—uncomfortably close, invading his personal space.

She said, "And now you're thinking about killing yourself, and making a public show of it. Do you think that's what Bonnie would want? Wouldn't she actually consider it pretty vulgar, a cheap way out?"

Shane's face reddened, and his lips drew back to reveal tightly clenched teeth.

I've got him now, Carly thought.

Maybe he would actually confess if she asked him directly—had he committed the murders? Were they part of his performance? Was he killing the women in preparation for his big finale—his own onstage suicide?

But before Carly could think exactly how to phrase the questions, Shane lunged forward and his hands clutched tightly around her throat. She automatically grabbed him by the wrists, but she couldn't pull his hands away.

Carly couldn't breathe, and whole world started to dissolve all around her.

*

Lyle gasped with horror.

"Carly!" he shouted.

He'd been standing among the spectators, watching with approval as his partner baited the creep on stage.

When Shane Crawford seized Carly by the throat, Lyle automatically reached for his weapon. But there were too many people in the way for him to fire, and he didn't draw the gun. He shoved several people out of the way as he rushed into the lighted area and grabbed the young man from behind, yanking him loose from his partner.

Carly tumbled onto the floor.

Lyle slung the perpetrator backwards, right into the arms of the two cops who had arrived with Sheriff Ketchum.

Lyle stooped down beside Carly, who was conscious but seemed stunned.

"Are you all right?" he demanded, taking her by the hand.

"Sure, Lyle," she croaked hoarsely. "Just help me get back on my feet."

"Like hell I will," Lyle said. "You need to lie down until we can get an ambulance here."

Carly snapped back at him sharply and with sudden clarity.

"Lyle, don't you dare call an ambulance. I mean it. The last thing I need right now is to go to a hospital."

"Well, lie down, at least."

"Huh-uh."

Pushing Lyle away from her, she struggled to her feet. She wobbled for a moment, and he reached out to steady her.

Carly brushed his arm aside and said, "I don't need help. I'm fine."

She means it, Lyle thought, starting to feel relief sinking in

The spectators were all on their feet and chattering in alarm, or perhaps in speculation that this was part of the performance. But they stood well back from the action. Lyle could see that two cops were escorting Shane Crawford out of the building.

"I feel like an idiot," Carly said, her voice still hoarse. "I should have seen that coming. I should have been able to fend him off."

Lyle was about to assure her she'd done just fine when Sheriff Ketchum stepped toward them.

Ketchum said to Carly, "Well, that was sure some unconventional detective work, Agent See. But why didn't you just draw your weapon and shoot the bastard?"

Lyle protested, "Not in the middle of all these people."

Carly added, "I knew you and the troops were nearby."

"All I can say is you got results," Ketchum said. "If that guy isn't the murderer we're looking for, I'll eat my badge. We'll get a confession or some physical evidence or both and tie the whole case up with a bow."

"I know where you can find physical evidence," Carly said. "There's a room in Crawford's house we weren't allowed to go into. His mother said Shane wouldn't like it."

Ketchum let out a grunt of satisfaction.

"Huh. Well, it doesn't matter whether he likes it or not. Now that he's assaulted a law enforcement agent, we've got all the probable cause we need to get a search warrant. I'll get right on the phone to a judge to get one ASAP."

Ketchum took out his phone and stepped away from Carly and Lyle.

Lyle said to Carly, "Maybe you should at least go back to the motel and get some rest."

"Not right now. I'm hungry."

*

A short while later, Lyle was looking at his stubborn younger partner over sandwiches on a Formica-topped table in a brightly lit café. Whatever discomfort she may have felt from nearly being strangled didn't seem to interfere with her appetite.

Small wonder she's hungry, Lyle thought. *It's been a long day.*

And it wasn't over yet. They were waiting for Sheriff Ketchum to fetch a search warrant so they could continue the investigation.

But Lyle found himself nibbling listlessly at his own sandwich. He didn't have much appetite at all. Although he was doing his best not to let his partner see it, he was still shaken over the performance artist's attack on her.

"You did some great work back there," he said.

"It wasn't so great. I was a dope for letting him get hold of me. I'd really hoped to get him to confess right then and there."

"Don't worry about that. We'll close the case before the day is over."

"Well, anyway, thanks for saving my life," Carly said, then took a bite of her sandwich.

Lyle squinted with slight surprise. For a moment he didn't know what she meant.

Oh, yeah, he realized. *I pulled the guy off of her.*

"That was nothing," Lyle said. "If I hadn't done it, somebody else would have. One of the cops, probably."

"Thanks anyway."

"Don't mention it."

She's tough as nails, I'll give her that, Lyle thought.

It was hard to believe she'd just recently been put on leave to recover from a shoulder wound delivered by a vicious killer with a dagger.

I guess I didn't need to worry about her being ready to get back to work, Lyle thought.

In fact, he was now wholeheartedly glad he'd let her talk him into joining him in Teapa. Her work back in that building just now had simply amazed him. It actually struck him as more than a little uncanny.

"How did you figure all that stuff out?" he asked Carly. "I mean, about how his twin sister committed suicide and all."

Carly shrugged as she ate.

"It was no big deal. That house was full of clues. Remember those family pictures with the boy and the girl? It was pretty obvious that Shane Crawford was the boy, and he'd had a twin sister, and that something bad had happened to her that Mrs. Crawford didn't want to talk about."

Lyle peered at Carly curiously.

"So you just made a wild guess that she'd committed suicide?" he asked.

Carly winced a little. Lyle saw that she was getting a bit uncomfortable with his questions.

"It made sense somehow," Carly said, suddenly sounding

somewhat evasive. "Somebody had gotten torn out of those family pictures—pretty obviously Mrs. Crawford's husband, the children's father. He must have done something pretty awful to get torn out like that."

"Something like abuse one of his kids?"

"Yeah. So it wasn't such a leap to guess Bonnie had committed suicide because of what she'd gone through."

Lyle didn't reply for a moment. The truth was, it did seem like a pretty remarkable leap, even for a detective as shrewd as Carly.

Finally, Lyle said cautiously, "Bonnie. That's odd. I don't remember hearing Mrs. Crawford mentioning her name."

Carly wiggled uneasily.

"I guess she must have said it," she replied slowly.

"Yeah, I guess she must have, and I missed it. I wasn't paying that much attention to what the two of you were talking about."

But Lyle remembered how Mrs. Crawford had shuddered when Carly had asked the girl's name. He was all but sure Mrs. Crawford hadn't spoken the name.

"I don't remember," the woman had said.

The woman had obviously been lying. But how had Carly guessed the name was Bonnie? Because judging from Shane's violent reaction, Bonnie must really have been the twin sister's name.

Carly doesn't want to tell me, Lyle thought.

That bothered him, as such things had sometimes bothered him before. He and Carly were normally open and honest about everything, the way good partners ought to be with each other.

And yet ...

He was sure that Carly was harboring some sort of a personal secret from him.

But what? he wondered as he kept eating his sandwich.

It was a longstanding mystery between them. Lyle supposed he could force the issue, demand that Carly tell him the whole truth about her occasional odd insights. But he respected her too much to do that.

She'll tell me in her own good time, he decided.

And if she didn't, maybe it really was none of his business.

Meanwhile, Lyle glimpsed Sheriff Ketchum entering the café. When he caught sight of Carly and Lyle, he chewed his tobacco with a widening smile and waved a piece of paper in the air.

"I've got it!" he said as he walked up to their table. "I've got a search warrant for Shane Crawford's house. My guys and I are heading over there right now. Would you two care to join the festivities?"

Lyle and Carly exchanged eager glances.

"Would we ever!" Carly exclaimed.

"We'll meet you there," Lyle told him.

Ketchum turned and headed on out of the café. Lyle and Carly took final hasty bites of what remained of their sandwiches, paid their bill, and hurried outside to their own vehicle.

Lyle felt his spirits rising.

This is it, he thought. *We're going to close this case.*

CHAPTER TWENTY ONE

Daylight was fading, and Carly had some hope that perhaps this case was also coming to an end.

Maybe we'll close this one before nightfall, she thought as her partner drove their vehicle back toward the Crawford house.

Even so, she was feeling uneasy about her recent conversation with Lyle. He'd been understandably curious about how Carly had known that Shane's twin sister had been named Bonnie and that she had killed herself.

Of course, Carly knew perfectly well that Mrs. Crawford hadn't mentioned her daughter's name. The woman hadn't even admitted that the girl in the photos was her daughter.

I lied to Lyle.

The thought made her cringe inside. Worse, she was sure Lyle knew she'd lied to him. It was an awful feeling. She was always careful to avoid talking about her gift with Lyle, but she'd seldom lied to him about it.

But what could she have told him instead? Was Lyle ready to hear the truth—that Bonnie herself had told Carly her name from the world of the dead?

Not an option, she thought.

And yet it was a reminder that there were unresolved issues in their relationship.

Maybe someday we can sort all that out.

As they pulled up to the curb in front of the Crawford house, Carly saw that Sheriff Ketchum and his two uniformed cops had already arrived and were standing beside their parked car.

Lyle grumbled to Carly, "I wish we could take care of this by ourselves."

"So do I."

They got out of the car and walked up to the waiting officers

Lyle told them, "Maybe you should let my partner and I go in first and get things started. The woman already knows us. She's liable to be more inclined to cooperate that way."

Ketchum spit out some tobacco and waved the warrant in Lyle's face.

"Not a chance. I'm the one who's got this piece of paper. You two just tag along and try to behave yourselves."

Carly shared a glance with Lyle. Her partner rolled his eyes with dismay.

"I just hope it's not a no-knock warrant," Lyle grumbled under his breath, so only Carly could hear.

Sheriff Ketchum was the first of the group onto the front stoop, and Carly was relieved that he didn't seem to be inclined to smash his way into the house. When he saw that the doorbell was marked "broken," he pounded on the door with the butt of his fist.

"Open up," he yelled. "This is the police."

As had happened when Lyle and Carly had been here before, there was no reply right away.

"Maybe nobody's home," Ketchum said.

"Try again," Lyle suggested.

Ketchum pounded again, and this time a familiar voice replied.

"Who is it?"

"This is Sheriff Ketchum, ma'am."

"I don't have any business with any sheriff."

"Are you Shane Crawford's mother?"

"Yeah."

The sheriff scoffed and said, "Well, I've got some business with you, ma'am. As a matter of fact, I've got a warrant to search these premises."

The woman's voice quavered with alarm now.

"A search warrant?"

"That's right, ma'am. Don't make this any harder than it has to be. Just let me and my people inside."

A silence ensued.

"I think you've got the wrong house," the woman said.

The sheriff spat into the yard and said, "Not if you're Mrs. Crawford, I don't. Now don't make me and my boys have to bust down this door."

Carly tensed up at the sheriff's command. Right now, the situation seemed likely to turn ugly and messy.

Then Carly heard the familiar sound of a chain rattling and a lock turning.

The door finally opened, revealing the house's wizened, inebriated inhabitant. Carly could tell by the veins in her face and her bloodshot eyes that Mrs. Crawford hadn't paused in her alcohol consumption since their earlier visit. Nevertheless, she seemed to have become markedly more alert, most likely on account of the sheriff's belligerent attitude.

The woman put her hands on her hips and glared at Ketchum.

"If you're looking for my son, he's not here," she said.

Ketchum scoffed again and said, "Yeah, we know that. We've already got him in custody."

Mrs. Crawford's eyes narrowed with surprised alarm.

"You've got him in *what?"*

"You heard me. He's in jail already."

The woman sputtered, "But—but—"

Ketchum ignored her perplexity and pushed his way past her into the house, followed by his two officers.

Lyle said to Carly, "We've got to try to keep this from getting out of hand."

"You two again!" the woman hissed at Lyle and Carly as they rushed in after the sheriff and his men.

It was apparent right away that Lyle's concern about Ketchum's methods was well-founded. The sheriff was pointing and giving orders to his two men.

"You guys start searching over this way. I'll head straight on ahead. Don't leave a drawer unopened anywhere in the house."

"Now hold on just a minute," Lyle said calmly. "We don't need to go tearing the whole place apart."

"Like hell we don't," Ketchum growled. "Don't try to tell me how to conduct a search."

Carly stepped in front of Ketchum.

"My partner's right," she said, pointing to the closed door she'd noticed earlier. "That's the room I told you about. That's where you'll find the evidence we're looking for."

"How do you know anything's in there?" Ketchum snapped.

"Just check it out and see for yourself," Lyle said.

As Ketchum took a few steps toward the door, Mrs. Crawford objected sharply.

"Shane won't like it if you go in there."

Ketchum smiled broadly and chuckled with satisfaction.

"He wouldn't, would he? Well, that's all the more reason for us to have a look-see."

Ketchum turned the doorknob and opened the door and flipped a wall switch to turn on an overhead light.

"Holy smoke!" he barked with surprise as he stepped on into the room. "Guys, get a look at this!"

Carly and Lyle managed to squeeze their way into the room ahead of the two officers.

Carly gasped aloud at what she saw.

There was no furniture in the room except for a small table and a narrow bed. But every inch of wall space appeared to be covered with images—hundreds, maybe even thousands of pictures that appeared to have been cut out of magazines and pasted everywhere. They were all of young women.

The pictures were many different sizes, but the women in them looked much alike, with the same buxom figures and curly, auburn hair. Carly immediately noticed a resemblance to the girl in the family photographs in the next room.

More disturbingly, each face was crossed out with thick red slashes of paint.

For a few moments, even Sheriff Ketchum seemed at a loss for words. Finally, he growled, "What do you suppose these all mean?"

Carly didn't reply, but she found it easy enough to guess. The slashes themselves seemed angry, as if to ask the same question posed by Shane Crawford's performance piece.

"Why aren't you dead?"

It seemed as though Shane was questioning the right of any of these women to live, now that his sister Bonnie was dead. She glanced at Lyle and saw that he was frowning as he contemplated the array of images.

One of the cops pointed to the table and said to the group, "Look here."

Carly saw a clutter of magazines on the table, in various states of being cut up. Similar images covered the tabletop. There were also a bottle of red paint, a wide paintbrush, and a jar of glue.

But what most caught Carly's attention was a quart bottle full of clear liquid surrounded by wads of cotton. When she leaned over it, she detected a very faint but familiar odor.

She murmured to Lyle, "Do you think … ?"

"Probably chloroform," Lyle murmured back with a nod.

Lyle turned to Ketchum and said sternly, "We need to talk to the suspect now. My partner and I will do the questioning."

"But—"

"No buts," Lyle said. "You called in the FBI for a reason. We're good at this. Just stay out of our way and let us do our job."

Sheriff Ketchum growled and shook his head, then stalked out of the room after his officers. As Carly and Lyle headed after him, Carly saw Mrs. Crawford standing in the living room, looking shocked and terrified.

"What's going on?" she demanded in a shaky voice. "What are you doing with my boy?"

"We've nailed him for murder," Sheriff Ketchum called back to her as he exited the house.

"Murder?" the woman said with a gasp. "I don't understand."

Carly and her partner continued on out of the house. She knew there was nothing she could say to Mrs. Crawford to put her mind at ease.

The poor woman, she thought as she and Lyle headed back toward their vehicle.

Shane's mother had already endured more than enough tragedies in her life. Although her son might be a murderous monster, he was apparently all the woman had left in the world.

What will become of her now? Carly wondered.

But she couldn't concern herself with that right now.

We've got a case to close, she told herself.

CHAPTER TWENTY TWO

This could be it, Carly told herself a short time later. *Depending on how Shane Crawford reacts to questioning.*

She and Lyle were standing in the police station's interrogation room, waiting for the suspect to be brought from his cell. They knew that Sheriff Ketchum and a couple of officers would be on the other side of the one-way mirror watching and listening. Carly hoped the cops would stay put and let them do their job.

But something else was actually troubling her mind.

When they'd been back at the Crawford house with all the pictures pasted to the walls, those images seemed to tell the whole story of Shane's murderous obsession. The bottle of chloroform appeared to seal the deal.

But now, Carly felt a nagging doubt. She didn't know why.

Did we get it wrong? she wondered.

Surely not.

And yet ...

But where was this spasm of doubt coming from? It was as if a barely audible voice was trying to tell her something important.

But whose voice was it?

Could Bonnie Crawford be reaching out to her again?

Carly shuddered as she remembered that powerful jolt she'd gotten from Shane's dead sister during his performance piece—the vivid mental snapshot of her hanged corpse. That visitation had made it possible to arrest Shane and search his home.

But now Carly wondered—had Bonnie shown Carly everything she had meant to show her?

Did she leave something missing?

Her thoughts were interrupted by the opening of the interrogation room door.

When the handcuffed Shawn Crawford was escorted in, he looked remarkably composed and even cheerful. He seated himself on one side of a battleship gray table, and Carly and Lyle sat down facing him.

"Oh, Agent See," he said with his usual winning smile. "I'm so glad to see you again. I'm afraid I was rather rude to you the last time we saw each other. That was wrong of me."

"You assaulted her," Lyle observed.

"Well, yes, I suppose I did at that. I'm sincerely sorry about that, Agent See. You were just doing your job, and I let you get the best of me. Please accept my apologies."

Carly knew better than to respond in kind. For one thing, she strongly sensed that his regret was just a tactic he used to reassert his dignity—a mask that was covering a lot of embarrassment and even shame.

Just let him feel insecure, she told herself. On their way to the station, Carly and Lyle had decided that she should take the lead in questioning this man. She didn't want him to get too comfortable, and she knew silence could work better than starting off with seriously confrontational questions.

Finally, she began with, "Tell me, Shane—do you mind if I call you Shane?"

"May I call you by your first name?"

"No."

Shane shrugged and chuckled.

"Fair enough. Go ahead and call me whatever you like."

"Then tell me, Shane. Where does one go to buy chloroform these days?"

"Oh, you found my bottle, did you? That means you must have gone into my private room."

"We had a warrant," Lyle put in.

"You needn't have bothered," Shane said. "I would have gladly given you permission to go inside and have a look around. It's not like I've got anything sinister to hide."

Carly restrained herself from scoffing aloud as she thought about all those unsettling pictures on the walls.

"Answer my question," Carly said.

"Oh, yes, about the chloroform. Well, you can buy it at just about any chemical supply store, but I didn't do that. I made it myself. The formula is simple, you can find it all over the internet—just one teaspoon of nail polish for every cup of bleach."

"What did you need a bottle of chloroform for?" Carly asked.

Shane shrugged and said, "Well, if you must know, I've got a substance abuse problem. I use chloroform to get high."

"I'm not buying that, Shane," Carly said. "I happen to know chloroform isn't much good for getting high. It's more likely to make you sick."

"Seldom doesn't mean never, does it? Metabolisms are different. Everybody has their own drug of choice. Mine happens to be chloroform. It stimulates my imagination, makes me more creative. And hey, it's not even illegal. Surely you don't plan to make a big deal out of it."

It was a lie, of course. But Carly knew better than to specifically mention how chloroform had been used to knock out the victims. The trick was to try to get Shane to tell them all about that with as little prompting as possible.

Lyle put in, "Let's just say we don't believe you."

Shane tilted his head and said, "Oh, you don't, do you? Well, I should have known you were too smart to fall for such a palpably false excuse. Yes, it's true I've got other reasons for keeping a bottle of chloroform."

"And what might that be?" Carly asked.

Shane chuckled and said, "Oh, no. I can't tell you that."

"Why not?" Carly asked.

Shane winked and his grin broadened.

"It's a professional secret."

Carly exchanged a fleeting glance with her partner at this provocative answer. Obviously, Shane was toying with them. But again, Carly got a nagging feeling they'd overlooked something.

Something about those pictures ...

Carly focused her mind back on the interrogation.

"Could you tell us where you were the night when Gemma Gosnell was killed?"

"About what time do you mean?"

"Between nine at night and dawn," Carly said.

"That's rather a long time. I suppose you also want to know where I was the night the other victim was killed—what was her name again?"

"Ariana Welch," Lyle said.

"And during approximately the same hours, I presume?"

"That's right," Carly said.

Shane drummed his fingers on the tabletop for a moment.

"I take it you talked with my mom," he finally said.

"Just answer my question," Carly said.

"I'm trying to, I really am. Where did Mom tell you I was during those two nights?"

She remembered what Mrs. Crawford had said when asked about

her son's whereabouts.

"I wouldn't know."

And of course, she'd been telling the truth. Shane knew he could count on his alcoholic mother not to remember whether she'd seen her own son coming or going.

He's tricky, she thought.

She knew it was a good thing she and Lyle were conducting the interrogation, and not the local Sheriff.

He'd make short work of Ketchum, she thought.

He might even wind up going free.

Carly said to Shane, "We want to hear what *you* have to say about where you were at those times."

Shane threw his head back and rolled his eyes and sighed.

"It's so hard to say," he said with wry irony. "Time flies so fast, doesn't it? At least it does for me. And I keep myself occupied in so many different ways. Even just last night seems like years ago. I'm afraid I can't help you."

Carly could hear her partner growl under his breath. She knew Lyle had a special sore spot for suspects who played taunting games like this.

Stay cool, Lyle, she thought.

Meanwhile, those nagging doubts of Carly's were starting to turn into something more serious.

Something is really wrong.

Was it possible that Bonnie was trying to reach her again? Was there something the dead girl desperately wanted her to know? Carly suppressed a shiver at the thought of having another psychic episode right here and now.

Again, she forced her attention back to the business at hand.

"You'd better start being straight with us," she said to Shane. "I don't think you understand the seriousness of your situation. This isn't just another one of your performance pieces we've got going on here."

"Oh, but I beg to disagree. Remember the topic of my lecture? 'Everything is theater.' That's true of what's going on between us right here and now. I for one am very excited about it! I've never performed in a police station before, let alone an interrogation room …"

Carly let him drone on, and she knew Lyle would do the same. It was a tried-and-true tactic to let suspects chatter like this during an interrogation. Shane's confidence was rising with every word he said, which made him all the more likely to trip up eventually.

But Carly was finding it harder and harder to focus on his spiel.

That nagging feeling had become much more than one of simple doubt now.

It is Bonnie, she realized.

She's really here.

She wants to tell me something.

But why couldn't Bonnie just say whatever she had to say outright? Something seemed to be blocking their communication.

What was the problem?

Then Carly remembered what had triggered Bonnie's previous visitation.

I'd touched her brother on the shoulder.

Would she need to do that again? This hardly seemed like the ideal situation for it.

I've got to try.

Fortunately, Shane had become so enchanted by the sound of his own voice that he didn't even notice Carly's hand creeping across the table until the tips of her fingers were very close to his.

Then their fingers touched.

Just as before, Carly felt an electrical charge.

And then she heard a young woman's voice speak loud and clear.

"My brother never killed anybody."

CHAPTER TWENTY THREE

Don't close your eyes, Carly told herself.

Don't show what you feel.

Even though the voice in her mind had startled her, she couldn't fall apart right now—not right here while interrogating a suspect, with Lyle at her side and cops watching through the one-way mirror.

She drew her hand slightly back, so her fingers were no longer touching Shane's. To her relief, the inner contact was not broken, and the intensity began to feel more manageable.

Shane didn't seem to have noticed either the touch or any change in her demeanor. He just kept droning on about the "performance" they were giving.

"We've even got an audience," he said, nodding toward the mirror. "I know perfectly well there are people watching and listening back there …"

Carly kept her eyes on the murder suspect in spite of the communications she was receiving from his dead sister. As long as Shane kept prattling about seeming irrelevancies, Carly hoped she had a chance to make some sense of this visitation.

Now the sound of his voice seemed to fade in Carly's consciousness. Her mind's eye was filled with images—a jumble that included those family photographs back at the Crawford house, the cut-out pictures on the wall, that bottle of chloroform …

But finally, one image imposed itself over all the rest.

It was Bonnie hanging by a belt from a door with a plastic bag on her face and …

That surgical mask.

The mask covering her mouth and nose really drew Carly's attention now.

For one horrible moment, she felt as though she herself were hanging in Bonnie's place, her head covered by the plastic bag as she struggled to breathe the scant air—a task that was all the harder because of an overwhelming smell, a mixture of sweetness and something antiseptic …

Chloroform, she realized.

Then the sensations suddenly ceased.

Carly's quick gasp of air didn't even slow Shane's pedantic chatter down.

"So like a great director once said, 'I can take any empty space and call it a bare stage.' This room is an empty space like any other."

Without saying anything aloud, Carly focused again on Bonnie's spirit.

"Talk to me, Bonnie," she thought silently. *"What did you do to yourself?"*

"I think you know," Bonnie murmured back in Carly's mind.

Things were beginning to make terrible sense to Carly. She continued to silently send out her thoughts to Bonnie's spirit, and Bonnie replied with a single repeated word.

"You used chloroform to commit suicide."

"Yes."

"You used it to sedate yourself while you hanged and suffocated yourself."

"Yes."

"And now—you're afraid your brother will do the same thing."

"Yes."

Carly now understood this visitation. Bonnie's spirit hadn't reached out to her because her brother was a murderer. Instead, Bonnie had reached out to Carly because she knew Shane was planning to commit suicide—whether publicly or in private didn't matter. She hoped Carly might keep that from happening.

"I don't know how I can help," she admitted silently.

"First stop him from being falsely accused. Only you can do that."

"But how do you know he's innocent?" Carly asked.

"Because I'm always with him. I never leave him. I watch over him. I know everything he does. And I want him to live—like we always said to each other when I was alive and we were kids, 'Stay in the game.'"

Bonnie's spirit seemed to recede from her consciousness, and once again Carly was aware of Shane having great fun with his impromptu piece of performance art.

This suspect was certainly egotistical and annoying.

But did that mean he was guilty of murder?

Not according to Bonnie, she thought. And that spirit had insisted that she knew everything that her living brother did.

Meanwhile, Shane sat back in his chair and rubbed his manacled hands together.

"So welcome to this play of mine! I hope you're enjoying playing the roles of antagonists in my story. You're playing your parts reasonably well. Agent See, you were particularly impressive earlier on, when you provoked me into attacking you. I suppose I'll face charges for that, won't I?"

Lyle said, "Oh, you're going to be charged with much more than that."

"So you say," Shane said. "But you've got me at a disadvantage there. I know nothing about these two murders you keep talking about."

"No?" Lyle said, taking out his cellphone. "Well, here's something that might jog your memory."

Carly knew what Lyle was going to do next. He brought up crime scene photos of the two bodies and showed them to Shane, eyeing him closely to gauge his reactions.

"Here's some of your best 'guerrilla theater' work," Lyle said.

Shane squinted slightly at the sight of the pictures.

"What makes you think this is *my* work?"

"Because all the evidence points in that direction," Lyle said.

Shane sat staring at the pictures for a moment. His expression was inscrutable. Carly could see that Lyle's attempt to provoke him into some sort of reaction had failed.

Finally, Shane spoke again in a tone that was considerably less playful and more down-to-earth than before.

"I'm not an idiot. I know when I need a lawyer."

"Are you sure?" Lyle said in a slightly facetious tone. "I would think a lawyer would spoil your performance. Cramp your style, maybe. Do you want somebody breathing down your neck constantly telling you to shut up?"

Shane's lip curled a little.

"I want a lawyer. I won't say another word until I get one. I want to go back to my cell until then."

"That can be arranged," Lyle said.

And sure enough, the officers who had brought Shane into the interrogation room entered again and escorted him out. Hardly was Shane gone before Sheriff Ketchum and the two other cops behind the one-way mirror came into the interrogation room.

"Too bad about him lawyering up like that," Ketchum said to Lyle and Carly. "For a moment there I thought he was going to confess everything. But I guess they all clam up and ask for lawyers when they know they're trapped but good."

"Yeah, that's what usually happens," Lyle said as he and Carly got up from their seats.

Ketchum chuckled heartily and said, "Well, no lawyer in the world can help him now. Anyone can see he's guilty as hell. It's just a matter of connecting the dots from here on out. Just ordinary police work, gathering a few last tidbits of evidence. Hardly something we need the FBI for. I expect you'll be heading back to Quantico now."

"I imagine so," Lyle said.

Carly and her colleagues were walking back through the police station now. Carly's mind was echoing with Bonnie's words:

"My brother never killed anybody."

And Carly had no reason to doubt the dead woman's spirit.

In a tentative voice, she said, "Sheriff Ketchum, what do you remember about Bonnie Crawford's suicide?"

The sheriff grunted, "To tell the truth, not a damned thing. Suicides are pretty run-of-the-mill among the artistic crowd here in Teapa. This isn't exactly the mental health capital of the world. Shrinks here have got a booming business."

Carly could tell by Lyle's sidelong look that he was wondering what had caused this query.

Carly said to the sheriff, "I wonder if you could do one little favor for me."

"Glad to oblige, I'm sure."

"Could you send me the case file on her suicide?"

Ketchum took out his cellphone and began to type in a text message.

"Sure, I'll put in the request right this second. Any particular reason you want to see it?"

Carly hastily thought of something to say.

"Oh, I'm just kind of curious about suicide cases, that's all."

Again, Carly noticed a wary look from Lyle, who of course knew that she had no particular curiosity about suicides. But she could count on him to not mention it, at least not yet.

"I'll have it zapped to you by email in just a jiffy," Ketchum said as he sent his text message. "I've got to say, the two of you did a fine job."

He patted Carly on the back in a condescending way and added, "Especially you, little lady. That was quite some maneuver you pulled back at the old Pastaworks building, getting him so riled up we just had to arrest him. Worked like a charm. I've got to say, I underestimated you. Whenever we get another serial killer here in Teapa, you'll be more than welcome to come and help us out. Of course, I hope that means *never.*"

The sheriff offered his hearty thanks and farewells as Lyle and Carly headed on out the door. Lyle laughed and gave Carly a playful nudge as they walked toward their vehicle.

"So what do you say, 'little lady?'" Lyle said. "Are you ready to get away from Teapa and its male chauvinist pig of a sheriff? Because I sure am. We can head right back to the motel and pack up our stuff and catch the next flight back to Quantico. Hey, why did you ask for that police report, anyway?"

Carly swallowed down a knot of anxiety as they got into their vehicle.

"Lyle," she said, "I think we arrested the wrong man."

CHAPTER TWENTY FOUR

Lyle felt a flash of irritation along with surprise at Carly's announcement.

"What do you mean, we got the wrong man?" he asked, keeping his voice calm.

"It's a feeling. A really strong one."

Just a moment ago, Lyle had been enjoying a sense of triumph over capturing a serial killer before he could kill again. Now Carly had deflated his mood in a just a few seconds.

Lyle shook his head and turned the ignition key.

"Well, I can't say I share your feeling," he said as the engine started and he pulled away from the curb. "The evidence is pretty solid. And anyway, Sheriff Ketchum politely showed us the exit just now. He made it clear we've got no further business here. We're on our way back to Quantico."

"I don't think we should leave Teapa tonight."

"Why not?" Lyle asked, driving in the dark toward their motel.

He waited as patiently as he could for her answer. Finally, Carly replied.

"I might be able to explain it better when I get the police report on Bonnie Crawford's suicide."

Lyle glanced over at his partner with disbelief.

"What does the girl's suicide have to do with anything?"

"Maybe nothing. Let's just wait and see, OK?"

Lyle fell silent again. He didn't feel like waiting, even though he had to admit that the wait shouldn't be very long. But the real question was, why should they wait here for Ketchum to send it to them?

"Let's just talk about this for a minute," Lyle said. "Surely we both can agree that Shane Crawford fits our profile perfectly. For one thing, he's sociopathic and completely narcissistic, with no regard for human life. He's also a megalomaniac with extreme histrionic tendencies. 'All the world's a stage' as far as he's concerned. And he's the star of the show."

"But none of that necessarily makes him a killer. What's his motive in killing these women?"

"He's obsessed with his sister's suicide, obviously. He's completely fixated on her. Like you told him during his performance, he blames himself for Bonnie's suicide, because he didn't defend her from their abusive father. But he represses that blame, turns it against other people—specifically women."

Lyle paused to think for a moment. Then he remembered the name of Shane Crawford's performance piece.

"'Why aren't you dead?' That's what he asked you. And that's the question he wants to ask women everywhere. Why is his sister dead while they get to live? His guilt got twisted into rage. And he started taking revenge by killing women. And showman that he is, he makes 'guerrilla theater' out of it."

A silence fell between Lyle and his partner. Lyle hoped that meant Carly was starting to see things his way.

Then Carly said, "Lyle, what about those pictures all over the walls of that room?"

"What *about* them? Don't they prove my point? Judging from the family pictures in the living room, all those women look like Bonnie did in her later teens—pretty and buxom. At some point he graduated from crossing out pictures to actually killing real-life women."

"But something's not right about that. Like you said, his sister and all the women in those photos were pretty and buxom. But the actual victims looked completely different. They were slim and willowy. Why wouldn't he seek out victims who looked like his sister?"

Lyle suppressed a discouraged sigh.

She's got a point, he admitted to himself.

Still, the man was a match in every other way, and he was obviously dangerous.

At that moment Carly's phone buzzed.

She looked at it and said, "I just got the email with the police report about Bonnie's suicide."

"What does it say?" Lyle asked.

Carly perused the report in silence for a few moments.

Finally, she murmured, almost too quietly for Lyle to hear, "It's just what I thought …"

"What do you mean?" Lyle asked.

Carly gave him a startled look, as if she hadn't meant to say those words aloud.

Then she began to explain, "Lyle, according to this report, Bonnie used chloroform to commit suicide. She hanged herself with a plastic bag over her head. But she also sedated herself to make it easier. She put on a surgical mask that held a rag soaked in chloroform over her mouth and nose. So she lost consciousness before she died."

"What does that prove?"

"Don't you see? Shane has made it no secret that he's planning his own suicide. In fact, people have been expecting him to make it part of his act. I think he expects to do it exactly like his sister did, as sort of a tribute to her."

Lyle squinted thoughtfully.

"So you don't think he was using the chloroform we found in that room to kill women?"

"No. I think he planned to use it when he killed *himself.*"

Lyle shook his head and said, "I think you're really reaching, Carly."

"Really? Then tell me why we didn't find any vecuronium in that room."

Vecuronium? Lyle wondered for a moment.

Then he remembered what the coroner had told them.

Oh, yeah. The anesthetic used to paralyze the victims.

"He might have been keeping it elsewhere in the house," Lyle said. "I can alert Sheriff Ketchum to do another search."

"He won't find any vecuronium. I'm sure of it."

"But Crawford fits the profile so perfectly."

"It only looks that way. He's really just a seriously screwed up actor-type. As far as he's concerned, getting arrested and being suspected of murder is the best publicity he could ever hope for. And he's not afraid of getting convicted, because he knows we can never prove something he never did. As far as he's concerned, getting charged with assaulting a law enforcement officer is well worth the hassle. In fact, it's just another great PR item."

Carly grunted and added, "But he's not as smart as he thinks he is. It hasn't occurred to him that he's eventually going to get charged with obstructing a police investigation. He's in a lot more trouble than he expected."

Lyle's brain clicked away as he tried to make sense of what Carly was saying.

"It's no good, Carly. Everything you're saying kind of makes sense, but only like some wacko conspiracy theory makes sense. It's way overly complicated. It's all logic and no evidence."

"So you still think Shane Crawford is our killer?"

"As a matter of fact, I do. More to the point, Sheriff Ketchum thinks so. And we're here in Teapa solely by his invitation and at his pleasure, and he just told us it was time to head back to Quantico. And that's what we're going to do. Tonight. When we get to the motel, we'll check for the next flights we can get out of the Albuquerque Airport."

A tense silence fell between Lyle and his partner.

Either she's mad at me or her feelings are hurt—or both, he thought.

But what was he supposed to do about that? As the senior partner, it was up to him and not her to make these kinds of decisions. And as far as he was concerned, his decision had been made.

Finally, Carly spoke again in a low voice.

"You can go back to Quantico tonight if you want to. I'm staying right here."

"What?"

"You heard me. You can't make me leave Teapa if I don't want to go."

Lyle sighed deeply and shook his head. He could order her to go, but if she still refused, he couldn't take her with him by force. Then he'd be faced with either ignoring or reporting her insubordination. Neither of those scenarios worked for him.

"Carly, you're just not thinking straight. I knew from the very start you were coming back to work too soon after getting stabbed like that. You needed more time to heal up."

"I've healed up fine. I don't need any more time. I know what I'm saying sounds kind of farfetched, and if you don't trust me about this, I guess I can understand. But I'm staying right here. If there's any way that I can keep anybody else getting killed, I want to do it."

They were pulling into the motel parking lot now. They said nothing for a moment as Lyle pulled into the parking space closest to their neighboring rooms and turned off the ignition.

"OK then, stay here," Lyle finally said. "You're right, I won't order you to go back to Quantico. But I'm pretty damn sure that this case is closed. You can't get in touch with Sheriff Ketchum about this. I don't want him to find out that either one of us is still here."

Carly's voice rose sharply.

"But I need to contact him. I need to let him know—"

"No, you don't. He'll have a fit if he finds out one of us is second-guessing him. He'll file a complaint about you, and it'll get you in a lot of trouble, and I won't be able to help you."

"But how am I supposed to do any investigating on my own?"

"I dunno. You'll just have to figure that out on your own. I'm sure you'll think of something. You're just full of creative ideas right now."

Lyle saw Carly's eyes soften with hurt. He wished he could take back that last remark.

There's no need to be mean about it, he thought.

"Just watch your step, OK?" he said. "Be careful."

Lyle got out of the car, and so did Carly. Before they started walking toward their rooms, Carly spoke again.

"Lyle, I just want you to know … I really, really hope I'm wrong about this. I really hope we've got the right man. If that turns out to be true, go ahead and give me a hard time about it. I can take it."

Lyle and his partner stared at each other over the top of their vehicle for a moment.

"I'll see you later," Carly said in a voice that sounded close to tears.

She strode ahead of him toward her room, unlocked the door, and disappeared inside.

Lyle found himself standing alone next to the car, feeling utterly miserable as he remembered the words he'd just said.

"You're just full of creative ideas …"

The last thing he'd wanted to do was hurt Carly's feelings. But of course, he'd done just that. Now he reprimanded himself for being impatient with her insistence that the case might not be closed.

Sometimes his young partner's mysterious certainty about her "strong feelings" really got to him. Lyle's own investigative skills were based on years of work with the Behavioral Analysis Unit. He knew that his methods were sound, that his thinking was solid and sometimes even brilliant. He trusted his results. But he was able to explain his observations to himself and even to others who had the capacity to grasp subtleties that he had learned to spot and analyze.

After four years of working together, he still didn't know how Carly reached some of her conclusions. In fact, he couldn't help but suspect there was more to her abilities than anyone could rationally account for. Occasionally she seemed on the verge of explaining something to him, but she always shied away.

Maybe someday, he thought.

That is, if she thinks it can *be explained.*

But tonight, he was tired of wondering about her odd notions. He wanted to feel good about the arrest they'd made. That man they had arrested certainly deserved to be locked up.

Lyle trudged toward his own room and went on inside. He sat down at the table and used his cellphone to look up flights out of the Albuquerque Airport. There was one he could catch pretty easily if he packed up and drove to the airport right now.

But his fingers faltered as he tried to make the reservation.

He found himself thinking about the last time he and Carly had been at odds like this. It was during the last case they'd worked on together—the one that had ended with Carly almost getting killed.

They'd arrested a serial murder suspect, and that time also Carly had doubted they had the right man.

"Lyle, I don't know ..." she'd said.

And like he had just now, Lyle had snapped at her.

"Kid, it's not up for discussion," he'd said.

The thing was, Carly had been right—they *had* gotten the wrong man. The real murderer had still been at large—and his next targeted victim had been Carly herself. Lyle's stubbornness had very nearly gotten Carly killed when she persisted in investigating on her own.

Lyle shuddered as he remembered how he'd arrived at the crime scene just in time to save Carly's life. It had come much too close to repeating one of the worst days of his career—Dawn Metcalf's shooting death. That earlier young partner had murmured deliriously with her last breath.

"Thanks, Lyle. You're always watching out for me."

Lyle felt a knot of guilt and grief rising up in his throat.

I can't risk losing Carly, he thought.

I just can't leave her here alone. The locals won't back her up.

Of course, if he was right and the killer had been caught, then Carly wouldn't be in any danger. But something more was nagging at his mind. Lyle simply had to wonder—was it possible that Carly was right?

Again?

While her theory struck him as strained and implausible, Carly's odd intuitive leaps often turned out to be completely correct. Would he be making a fatal mistake if he didn't give her the benefit of the doubt?

Lyle drew a deep sigh.

It wouldn't kill me to stay in Teapa another day, he thought.

So instead of booking a plane reservation and checking out of the motel, Lyle settled in for the night. He thought about giving Carly a call but didn't want to risk another confrontation. If she lashed out at him, he might well lash out at her in return.

Instead, he typed a text message.

I'll stay till tomorrow too.

He sat staring anxiously at the message, wondering whether Carly would respond. For all he knew, she might just tell him to go back to Quantico and leave her the hell alone.

But then the answer appeared.

I'm glad.

Lyle smiled. Then he typed another text.

Sorry I got grouchy.

Then came another reply.

You had your reasons. Goodnight.

Lyle pushed his phone away, feeling better now. Then he got up and went to the bathroom to take a shower. As he stood under the hot, steaming water, new worries started to creep into his mind. What could he and Carly hope to do tomorrow without provoking Sheriff Ketchum's ire?

We've got to tread lightly, he thought.

But he was also bothered by a much more dire concern.

If Carly *was* right, the killer was still out there.

And for all Lyle knew, he'd already picked out another victim. Maybe he had even killed again.

CHAPTER TWENTY FIVE

Vera Dunn awoke with a splitting headache.

She opened her eyes but couldn't see anything at all.

Why? she wondered.

Her bedroom was never pitch dark like this. Even with the blinds down, light from the street spilled in through the window.

Then she realized that nothing felt right. She had no pillow under her head. Instead of a mattress, the surface under her body was uncomfortably hard and solid.

She wasn't at home in bed.

Was she ill? Had some kind of stroke rendered her helpless? Could this be a hospital? She was finding it hard to think things out, and she could feel fear rising.

Then Vera tried to shift her position and discovered that her wrists and ankles were restricted by what felt like leather straps. She realized that the reason she couldn't see anything was because of something covering her eyes.

Memories burst into her confused mind. People all over Teapa had been talking all day long about the weird murders of two women. They had been abducted straight off the street.

That can't be what's happening, she thought.

She had been so careful last night after leaving the art class where she'd been posing as a model. A friend, a guy from the class, had driven her straight home, then had watched to make sure she got safely inside her front door before he'd driven away.

And then she'd turned on the living room light and …

And then what?

Her memory of what happened right then was strangely foggy.

Something happened.

One image came back to her—a living room window had been standing wide open, when she knew perfectly well it had been shut earlier on.

I should have locked it.

It had seemed like a small lapse.

Now patchy memories swarmed through her mind.

Hands on her arms … someone seizing her from behind … a damp cloth covering her nose and mouth … a sickening taste and smell, at once sweet and sharply bitter, and then …

Nothing.

Except that now she could feel a hand brushing her hair.

She shivered violently.

A man's voice spoke from so close by that she could feel his breath on her cheek.

"How are you doing, Vera?"

She let out a gasping cry.

"Oh, I'm afraid you have a headache," the man said with syrupy mock-sympathy. "That often happens after a dose of chloroform."

Chloroform, Vera realized.

That's what had been used to render her unconscious.

How stupid I was not to lock that window.

Then she felt his fingers all over her face, smearing some kind of oil all on her skin, even under the blindfold that covered her eyes.

But why?

When he'd finished with this weird task, the man said, "This will hurt only for a moment."

"Let me go," Vera whimpered.

Then she felt a sharp pain of a hypodermic needle in the crook of her arm. A nauseous dizziness swept over her.

Then the man chuckled cruelly.

"Actually, I'm afraid you might find this rather unpleasant."

Suddenly she felt her whole body go slack and her sensations becoming dull. She heard a buzzing sound, and although she could barely feel it, she was aware of something moving across her scalp.

An electric razor, she realized.

He was shaving the hair off the front of her head.

But why?

She struggled to ask what he was doing, but her voice wouldn't come. Her lips could no longer move.

Finally, the man spoke.

"Look at me, Vera."

With those words he removed the blindfold from her eyes, and she found herself staring up into a smiling face.

"Mine will be the last face you ever see," the man said.

Then he began to pour something onto her face. It was thick and pasty, and she was helpless as it spread over her eyes and her cheeks and her mouth and nose.

Vera couldn't move, and she couldn't breathe.

I'm going to die right here and now, she realized.

CHAPTER TWENTY SIX

Carly was surrounded by pitch darkness.

She heard a weeping woman's voice calling out from nearby.

"You've got to stop him."

Carly felt a deep tingle of déjà vu.

The situation seemed uncannily familiar ...

Of course, *she realized.*

My dream last night.

My *lucid* dream.

She was having the same dream again—or another very much like it.

"You've got to stop him," the voice said again.

"Stop who?" Carly asked. "How can I help you?"

"You can't help me," the unseen woman said with a sob. "It's too late to help me."

Carly shuddered deeply at those words. She knew they could only mean one thing.

He's already killed again.

Another woman was dead at his hand and reaching out to her now.

The woman added, "But you can still save a life. You can stop him before he does it again."

With her arms outstretched, Carly groped her way through the darkness.

"I'll stop him, I promise," she said. "But I need your help. I need you to tell me everything you can about him."

The woman's voice heaved with gasping sobs.

"How can I talk about something I don't understand?"

"You've got to try. Can you show me where you ... ?"

Carly struggled to think of what questions to ask.

"Where were you killed?

"Where are you now?"

A light as red as fire glowed for a moment, revealing shapes she couldn't identify at first. Then she recognized a long table with lumps of some material scattered on it.

Clay, *she thought.*

Was it the kind of clay used to pose the victims' bodies in those grotesque positions?

Other objects on the table could be tools of some kind. For a moment she glimpsed coils of something hanging above the table.

Heavy wire?

A workshop?

The victim was surely trying to show her something, but Carly saw no clue to where this was or even exactly what it was.

For a moment, she saw a pair of eyes glaring at her.

His eyes, *she knew.*

As she took another step forward, darkness closed around her again. Had she seen all that this spirit could manage to show her?

Carly kept moving forward through the dark, and then, just as in her earlier dream, her fingers came upon warm flesh wet with tears. It trembled under her touch.

Her face, *Carly realized.*

She was touching the most recent victim's face.

But this face was becoming harder to her touch. Finally, it was as hard and lifeless as a rock. Then it became warmer, as if the unseen woman had a fever. In another instant it became searing hot, and Carly yanked her fingers away.

The face started to sparkle in the darkness, then to fill up like a clear, glassy container with some sort of glowing yellow-white liquid. She heard a hot hissing noise.

Finally she found herself staring at a shining, eyeless visage very much like the one she'd glimpsed at the morgue.

"Where can I find him?" Carly shouted. "How can I stop him?"

The dead woman's spirit gave her no answer.

A series of sharp sounds interrupted the dream. It took Carly a moment to realize that someone was knocking on her motel room door.

That can only be Lyle, she realized.

And that can only mean ...

She scrambled out of bed and opened the door.

Sure enough, Lyle was standing there in the early morning light, looking rather shaken.

"I just got a call from Sheriff Ketchum ..."

Lyle's voice faded.

"There's been another murder, hasn't there?" Carly asked, although she was already sure of the answer.

They hadn't caught the killer after all.

Lyle nodded and told her, "We've got to get over to the crime scene right now." Then he added, "We need to hurry. I'll wait in the car."

Fully awake now, Carly realized she was still in her pajamas.

She closed the door, then dashed around her room and bathroom, tying her hair back and throwing on some clothes. Then she went out and joined Lyle in their vehicle.

"What did the sheriff tell you when he called?" Carly asked as Lyle started to drive.

"Nothing, except that there's another victim. A woman's body was found early this morning in Cottage Grove Park. Same MO."

"The third in that same area."

Lyle added with an ironic scoff, "Ketchum told me he needed us to fly back from Quantico right away. He seemed understandably surprised to hear we'd never left."

After a few moments of silence, Lyle spoke again.

"I feel like an idiot."

"Why?"

"I shouldn't have pushed back so hard against you last night. I should have trusted your instincts."

"You had good reason to doubt me. My instincts might have been wrong."

"Yeah, but they weren't, and I'm sorry."

"It's OK, Lyle. You did stay anyway. And I'm glad you did. Whatever we're dealing with, I wouldn't want to spend all morning waiting for you to fly back to Teapa. Thanks for listening to me."

The sun was rising by the time they arrived at Cottage Grove Park. Several police vehicles, the coroner's van, and a couple of news vehicles were parked at the park's edge. Carly saw that there was considerably more activity than there had been at the crime scene the day when she and Lyle had arrived.

The Stetson-wearing Sheriff Ketchum slouched toward them.

"You two must have teleported from Quantico," he said, spitting a stream of tobacco.

Lyle began, "It's like I said on the phone—"

Ketchum interrupted, "Yeah, yeah, I know, you never left Teapa. There's something odd about that. I seem to remember telling you yesterday your work here was finished, didn't I? Yeah, I'm pretty sure that's what I said. But you stayed over anyway. And now someone else is dead. It's almost enough to make a lawman feel downright suspicious."

He spat again and added with a smirk, "Never mind, I don't reckon you're persons of interest. And it turns out I need you more than I expected, so … well, thanks for staying, I guess. Come on, let me show you what's what."

Ketchum led Carly and Lyle along a walking path through the park as the morning sunlight shimmered among the trees. He pointed to the nearby playground, where a couple of his cops were questioning a pair of disconsolate-looking young women who were sitting on a swing set.

"Those two girls found the body. They're photography students, and they came here bright and early to take some nice pictures of the park at dawn. I talked to them just now. They're pretty traumatized, but they don't know anything useful."

Carly was sure Ketchum was right about that. Unless the witnesses had gotten here before the murderer had left, they couldn't have seen anything to report. And they certainly couldn't be suspects. Carly and Lyle were both sure the murderer was male.

Up ahead in the center of the park, Carly saw that the gazebo was the hub of the current activity. Cops were busily putting up police tape around the structure to keep the growing group of gawkers and reporters away.

As they neared the gazebo, Ketchum spoke in a tone of uncharacteristic regret.

"I can't believe we let it happen right here in the same park again. Yesterday I'd recruited a team to stay out here all night and make sure nothing happened. But once we had that joker Shane Crawford in custody …"

Ketchum's voice faded, then he added, "Well, I called them off. We let our guard down, damn it. And the killer's definitely one brazen character, I'll give him that. He must have hauled the body out here in the dead of night without being seen."

As they neared the gazebo, the body itself came into view, positioned right in the middle of the structure. Standing in the gazebo and leaning against a railing was Roger Poole, the county coroner. He was smoking a cigarette and looking down at the corpse with what appeared to be mild curiosity.

Carly felt a strange tingle as she, Lyle, and Sheriff Ketchum mounted the steps to the platform and got a closer look at the body. Like the other two corpses, this one was weirdly positioned, with large mounds of clay supporting the head, right arm, and right leg. Also like the others, the woman's head had been shaved far back onto the scalp.

"So what do you make of this young lady?" Poole asked as Carly and her colleagues approached. "What kind of pose do you take this for? It looks to me like she's kicking a football."

At a glance, Carly almost agreed. The woman's right arm was thrown backward, the left arm was high above her head, and her right leg was raised high as if kicking something.

Carly felt that tingle turning into a flash of déjà vu. Even so, she was sure she hadn't seen this body in a dream or a vision …

Then it dawned on her.

With a gasp, she told Lyle, "I know what the poses are. I've seen this one before."

CHAPTER TWENTY SEVEN

Carly saw the surprise on her partner's face. In fact, she felt a bit shocked herself.

Lyle sounded dubious when he asked, "What do you mean, you've seen this pose before?"

Am I wrong? she wondered.

She was relieved that Sheriff Ketchum and the coroner were in mid-conversation and hadn't overheard her comment. Instead of replying to Lyle, Carly stepped closer for a better look at the woman's body, still held in place by those lumps of clay.

She was sure.

No mistake.

Finally, Carly told Lyle, "I can't exactly explain it. I don't quite understand it myself. But we've got to head back to the car. We've got to go somewhere to check something out. Right now."

Lyle reminded her, "We just got here."

Carly stifled a sigh. He was right, of course.

She said, "I understand. Just give me the keys and I'll go there. If it's nothing, I'll come right back."

Lyle shook his head and let out a snort of disagreement.

"Huh-uh," he said.

Carly felt a stab of anxiety.

Are we going to get into an argument—again?

Then Lyle added, "I'll drive."

As the two of them headed down the steps of the gazebo, Sheriff Ketchum called out, "Hey, where do you think you're going?"

Lyle called back over his shoulder, "We're just checking out a lead."

"Care to let me in on it?"

"We will if it amounts to anything," Lyle replied.

"But what are we locals supposed to do in the meantime?" Ketchum asked with a note of sarcasm in his voice.

Lyle turned toward him with his hands in his pockets.

"Do you know the dead girl's name?"

"Yeah, she had I.D. on her. It's Vera Dunn."

Lyle grunted in reply, "Well, you know the drill. Get things started. Talk to friends, family, and everybody else who might have any idea what happened to her. Or why."

He started away again, then turned back and added, "And don't let Shane Crawford go loose. Even if he didn't kill anybody, his showboating set back our investigation and probably got this girl killed. He needs to get the book thrown at him."

"Right," Ketchum called out. "Just don't you two go flying back to Quantico, d'you hear?"

"Don't worry about that," Lyle yelled back with a wave.

As they hurried back through the park, Lyle told Carly, "That ought to keep Ketchum and his guys busy. But if this one is like the other two, the girl's family and friends won't know anything helpful. So when are you gonna tell me what this is all about?"

Carly tried to find the right words to explain, but all she really had were mental images. Her mind kept visualizing all three of the posed corpses. And now the last one suddenly seemed to have an important connection with something she'd seen yesterday. She knew there was nothing supernatural or paranormal about the feeling she had right now—no communication from the dead, just an observation built from bits and pieces of recent experience.

Sometimes a hunch is just a hunch, she thought.

When they got to the car, Carly said, "I'll drive. I know where we need to go."

Lyle handed her the keys without comment.

She navigated to the downtown area and parked near a gallery called Birch Street Artworks. Yesterday, she had noticed the sculptures on display in the window when she and Lyle passed by on their way to Shane Crawford's ill-fated performance piece. Now she rushed to that window to see if she remembered it right.

The same small reproductions were still on display—the Remington cowboy on a bucking horse and Rodin's *The Thinker* among several other cast metal figures.

And I was right!

"Does anything in there catch your eye?" Carly asked Lyle, who had stopped beside her.

For a moment Lyle silently scanned the work in view.

"My God," he said in a stunned voice.

Carly wasn't surprised by Lyle's reaction. It really was a startling sight—actually strangely frightening.

Standing among the other replicas was a small sculpture of what appeared to be a petit ballet dancer, posing with her left hand above her head and her right leg extended in a sort of kicking motion.

"It's exactly the same pose as today's victim," Lyle added.

"I'm sure of it. I think it's a reproduction of a sculpture by Edgar Degas, the Impressionist."

"Yeah, I remember him, the French guy who did lots of paintings of ballerinas. I think you're right. But what does it mean?"

"I don't know. Let's go inside and ask some questions."

Carly and Lyle continued on inside the gallery, where they were greeted by a chubby, cheerful, colorfully dressed young woman.

"How may I help you today?" the woman asked.

Carly and Lyle produced their badges.

Lyle said, "I'm FBI Special Agent Lyle Ramsey, and this is my colleague, Special Agent Carly See."

The woman's eyes widened with alarm.

"The FBI! Goodness! Why are you … ?"

Her voice faded for a moment, then she said, "Wait a minute. Does this have something to do with those murders everybody is talking about? I heard there was another victim this morning. And in our peaceful little town! It's all so terrible! But why are you here?"

"We just want to ask you a few questions, ma'am," Carly said.

The woman shrugged nervously and said, "I can't imagine why, but … well, I'll do whatever I can to help. My name is Sierra Smith, and I own this gallery."

Lyle asked, "Do you have any idea who might be committing these murders?"

"No, none at all."

"Are you sure?" Carly asked. "Have you had any unsettling interactions with people lately? Has anyone come in here lately that struck you as suspicious? Or threatening?"

"Oh, Lord no," Sierra said with a slight laugh. "I'd definitely notice anyone the least bit odd. You see, I don't sell anything but reproductions here, no originals. Which means my clientele consists entirely of out-of-towners—tourists, and very ordinary, boring tourists at that. Anybody weird would definitely stand out."

Pointing toward the window, Lyle asked, "Has anybody shown any particular interest in that little dancer over there?"

"The Degas reproduction, you mean? Well, yes, those little figures are rather popular. I've sold a couple of others during recent months."

Carly exchanged a glance with Lyle.

"Why bought them?" Lyle asked Sierra.

The gallery owner said with a shrug, "Out-of-towners, as usual. A couple from Pennsylvania came in here, oh, two months ago, I think. They were vacationing with their 12-year-old daughter, who they said wanted to be a ballet dancer. So they bought one of the figures for her." She thought for a moment, then added, "The other was bought about a month ago by an elderly woman from Oregon."

Not exactly potential suspects, Carly thought.

She was sure Lyle was thinking the same thing.

Carly asked, "Were those the only customers who bought these figures recently?"

"Yes, I'm sure of it. Frankly, I don't like these Degas knockoffs at all. I'd rather not carry them. They give me the creeps."

"Really?" Lyle asked. "Why is that?"

Sierra smiled slightly, as if considering how best to answer his question.

She finally pointed out three pictures on display that were obviously reproductions of Degas paintings. Carly was sure she'd seen them many times before. All of them showed young female ballerinas in various stages of practice and rehearsal.

"What do you think of these?" Sierra asked. "How do they strike you?"

"The artist must have been fond of pretty young dancers," Lyle said.

But why would that drive anyone to kill? Carly wondered.

Sierra's smile looked more ironic now. She pulled down a coffee-table-sized book from a nearby shelf titled *The Works of Edgar Degas.* She set it down on a nearby table and opened it up to a full-page illustration of a sculpture that Carly instantly knew she'd seen somewhere before—a young ballerina wearing a buttoned, bare-shouldered bodice and a tutu. Her head was tilted back, one leg was extended forward, and her arms were held behind her back.

"Does this one also strike you as a pretty girl?" Sierra asked.

"Why wouldn't it?" Lyle asked.

Sierra fell silent for a moment.

Then she said, "This piece is called *Little Dancer Aged Fourteen.* It's the only sculpture Degas ever exhibited during his lifetime, in 1881. There was a good reason for it being his last. It wasn't received well. The public and many critics were horrified by it. They found it shocking and ugly."

"Why?" Lyle asked, his forehead crinkling with curiosity.

Carly wondered the same thing.

"Probably because Degas meant it to looking shocking and ugly," Sierra said, pointing to the photo. "For one thing, he made it out of materials no sculptor would normally use—wax and clay and wood chips shaped over a lead pipe frame, with real hair, a real bodice and tutu, and real ballet slippers. And Degas deliberately exaggerated the girl's features to make her look unattractive. More than unattractive—sinister, even degenerate."

"She doesn't look that way to me," Carly admitted.

"No, but her original viewers would have thought so. The pseudoscience of that day held that a person's features revealed their character. Notice how this girl's skull is flattened and her chin is stretched. Critics described her as a 'flower of precocious depravity' and as having a 'profoundly heinous character.'"

Carly herself was shocked now.

"But she's just a girl!" Lyle exclaimed quietly.

"Degas wouldn't have seen her that way," Sierra said. "He was well-known during his life to harbor a deep hatred of women. Some biographers think it was because he caught a sexually transmitted disease in a brothel as a young man. He despised women ever after that. He never had intimate relationships with them for the rest of his life."

Carly felt a shiver of comprehension slowly coming over her.

She said to Sierra, "You said this was the only sculpture Degas exhibited in his lifetime. But what about that little dancer in the window?"

Sierra nodded and said, "An excellent question. It's only a reproduction, of course—and not an especially faithful one at that. During the last part of his life, Degas created about 150 small sculptures like this."

"Can you show us pictures of some of them?" Lyle asked.

"Certainly," Sierra said, turning the pages of the enormous book.

She quickly came to a spread showing a group of sculptures that she described as seven dance positions.

Carly gasped, and she heard Lyle's quick intake of breath.

The figure in the window was among the pictures, but two others were also familiar. One showed a girl with her hands on her hips and one leg extended forward. Another seemed to be caught in mid-stride as one arm pointed forward and the other trailed behind her.

Those two poses were identical to the positions of the first two murder victims.

The killer had arranged three victims to match sculptures in these photographs.

Sierra paused and looked up at the agents curiously.

"But I can't imagine what any of this has to do with your case," she said.

Carly looked at Lyle, and he at her, as if to silently ask each other, *Should we tell her?*

They exchanged a nod of agreement.

Lyle said, "The killer is posing the corpses of his victims in some of these positions."

Sierra gasped aloud.

"How horrible! But why?"

"That's what we need to understand," Carly said.

"Tell us about the girls that Degas used as models," Lyle said. "Why would anyone have thought they were depraved or degenerate?"

"Well, they certainly came from the lowest part of society. The girls who danced with the Paris Opera were desperately poor. They sometimes started dancing at the age of eight, and they worked 10 to 12 hours a day. When they turned 13, they began to live double lives as dancers and sex workers. Wealthy male opera patrons would wait in the wings during performances to take advantage of the girls' desperation and vulnerability."

Carly felt chilled at what she was hearing. Suddenly, these familiar images of "pretty dancers" looked more sinister than she'd ever imagined.

Sierra continued, "And of course, they got diseases and lived short, miserable lives. Degas seems to have positively enjoyed the girls' plight. The face of girl who posed for *Little Dancer Aged Fourteen* is pitted with signs of disease for everyone to see. He called his models 'little monkey girls' and considered them to be barely human. And in his artworks, he tried to capture them at their most miserable and degraded—as he put it, 'cracking their joints,' and 'in the state of animals cleaning themselves.'"

Sierra shuddered a little, then shrugged and said, "I hope this is helping."

"I hope so too," Lyle said. "Tell us more about these little statues."

"Well, nobody even knew they existed until after Degas died in 1917. And by then, they weren't in any condition to be shown in public. Degas had probably never even meant them to be displayed. He'd made them out of wax, clay, scraps of fabric, and even wine corks, sort of like miniature versions of *Little Dancer*. He shaped these materials over wire frames—apparently for his own viewing only. They were in a terrible state of disrepair by the time they were found, and some of them were already ruined."

Sierra added with a scoff, "But of course, people are always eager to make money off of a dead artist's work. So his heirs made casts of the originals to make bronze copies of them to sell to the public. The ones you can buy in galleries like mine are copies of copies—or even copies of copies of copies. As artworks, I'll have to admit, they're really pretty much worthless."

She shrugged again and added, "But people love to buy them." she added.

Carly felt a new realization starting to take shape.

"How are these metal copies made?" she asked Sierra.

"In foundries. By pouring molten bronze into plaster casts."

At the mention of molten bronze, Carly flashed back to the dream she'd awoken from this morning—a human face becoming harder to the touch, then hotter and hotter, and then sparkling and glowing as the face filled up with blazing liquid, and that terrible hissing noise …

A foundry! she thought.

CHAPTER TWENTY EIGHT

The man couldn't help being a bit amused to see the awkward shape that the coroner's team was hauling away on a gurney.

Still in rigor mortis, he realized.

He found it intriguing that the human body became rigid for at least a few hours after death. The white sheet formed a tent-like shape over the corpse because of the outstretched positions of its limbs. It might as well be an actual statue of some kind.

How appropriate, he thought.

He wondered if anybody had yet caught on to the meaning of those positions, or whether he would eventually have to explain them.

Of course, his own creations were going to be more permanent.

He reminded himself to move along.

Don't want to attract attention, he thought.

Not that there was much danger of being noticed. He was sure he looked just like the other gawkers standing across the street from Cottage Grove Park to watch the police activity. Nevertheless, he began to work his way through the crowd. As he moved among the others, he overheard bits of conversation.

"Another murder," someone nearby said.

"I thought they had the killer in custody."

"Yeah, that's what I heard last night. I guess they turned out to have the wrong guy."

"You'd think they wouldn't make a mistake like that, with FBI agents on the case."

"Is the FBI here?"

"Two agents, they say."

FBI agents! the man thought as the body was loaded into the van.

It was the first he'd heard of that. Apparently, the local police had found him to be too formidable and elusive an adversary to deal with on their own. They'd called for more expert assistance. He felt an unbidden flush of pride before reminding himself of his true goal.

I'm not some common murderer.

I have a greater purpose.

He was following in mighty footsteps. Only a small number of men over the centuries had fully recognized the profound moral and physical inferiority of some who thought of themselves as equals. Despite women's superficially human characteristics, a few men like himself had always known they were a separate, aberrant species—necessary for procreation, of course, but worthy of being treated no better than livestock.

Those visionary men had done their best to alert their fellow males to the importance of complete female subjugation. It was his great task to continue their work.

I will do Degas proud.

He was especially devoted to the legacy of the esteemed artist who had left his brilliantly sculpted menagerie of hideous dancing "rats" and "little monkeys" so woefully unfinished. The only sculpture Degas had ever fully realized at its full scale, *Little Dancer Aged Fourteen,* had been mocked and reviled by an uncomprehending world. His public was uncomfortable with the master's depiction of reality.

Misinterpretations had grown even worse in more recent times. Rather than better understanding the master's work, an adoring audience had come to think of his ballerinas as pretty images of innocent young dancers.

But they won't be so mistaken for much longer.

The man was determined to continue Degas's visionary work and make the world take heed. He'd complete a monument to female inferiority that would stand for as long as *man*kind walked the earth. The women he chose ought to feel honored to help him do it, if only they were capable of understanding.

Meanwhile, judging from what people were saying nearby, circumstances were changing faster than he'd counted on.

Someone was already arrested!

He hadn't expected that. He breathed a sigh of relief that the authorities had caught the wrong man. Otherwise, his work might have been interrupted long before it was complete.

But events were moving quickly, and he had to move quickly too. He had to admit he'd been caught off guard. He'd only used three women so far and he needed seven in all to complete the sequence of Degas figures that he wanted to reproduce in his own style. He'd thought he could wait another day to claim his next victim, but now he needed to speed up his schedule. Although he had several candidates in mind, he hadn't even decided who it would be, much less made a plan to abduct her.

But who would he choose?

As if in reply, he heard the grumble of a little engine nearby. He turned and saw a helmet-clad young woman approaching on a motor scooter.

He recognized her immediately with a smile.

Nancy somebody, he thought.

Her last name was Raul or Ruhl or Rahl or something like that.

Not that it really matters.

She was, in fact, one of the women he'd been considering for his next effort. But he'd all but given up hope of finding a way to abduct her. Most of the time, she was surrounded by friends, chatting and laughing away as though she was of some significance in this world. And she apparently didn't live right here in town. He'd never figured out how to catch her alone.

Was that situation about to change?

He scarcely dared to hope so.

She drove right past him without giving him so much as a glance. Not that she didn't recognize him. He was sure she did.

She's just ignoring me—like they all ignore me.

For his own part, he felt ashamed to experience a spasm of sexual attraction toward her, like he did toward many of her sex. But temptation was never really an issue for him. He'd long ago given up making any serious erotic advances toward women. They seemed almost conspiratorial in their determination to reject him.

And a good thing, too, he thought.

Women seemed to be gifted with a unique natural instinct that warned them of his true nature—that he was, in fact, their natural predator, and they were his potential prey. With their animal-level intelligence, they'd been smart enough to reject him—and he'd been lucky. If he'd fallen into the clutches of even one seductress, he might have been doomed to live forever in their vile bondage.

Like so many other men.

Watching as the woman's scooter braked at a stoplight, he remembered meeting her during a still-life drawing class a few days ago. He'd complimented her on what was actually a clumsy charcoal drawing of a couple of wine bottles and a wooden bowl full of fruit.

"Very pretty," he'd said, looking over her shoulder as she worked.

She'd turned her head and glared at him as if he'd insulted her, then resumed drawing without saying a word.

At least she could have thanked me, he thought.

But no, she'd had to make a show of snubbing him. He couldn't blame her for that, really. It had been a reflex on her part. She'd felt compelled not to betray the slightest bit of interest in him—much less any hint of the awe she'd surely felt in his presence.

The light stayed red for what seemed an especially long time, and he was able to study the woman's figure with considerable attention. Like the others he'd chosen, she was small, slender, and limber—very much like the little dancing whores Degas had portrayed.

In fact, he was able to visualize the exact pose he would use her for if chance permitted it. One of Degas's "little monkeys" was positioned at the climax of a great arabesque, standing on one leg like while thrusting another backward and bending her torso far, far over at the waist with arms stretching out from her shoulders, making her look like a swooping bird of prey. It was one of the poses he'd already been planning to use.

Yes, that would suit her well, he thought.

But was he going to get a chance to fulfill this flash of inspiration? For a moment, it looked unlikely. The light turned green, and the woman named Nancy continued through the intersection on her scooter.

But the man's heart quickened as she switched on a turn signal, slowed down, and turned into a nearby parking garage. Apparently, she was stopping in the neighborhood to do some shopping.

Perfect! The man thought.

More than perfect!

Providential!

Most of the time, the man was disinclined to believe that his actions were guided by destiny. But at times like now, there could be little doubt that fate itself was on his side, helping him along in his vital mission.

He started walking toward his own parked car, his brain clicking away as he planned what to do next. He would drive his car into the garage, which wouldn't be very full at this time of day, and park as near as he could to the woman's scooter.

Of course, he'd have to be careful of security cameras, but he felt sure that he could render himself unrecognizable with sunglasses and a hat. And in his car, he had all the materials he needed to carry out the abduction, including a bottle of homemade chloroform.

He thought ahead with pleasure. As soon as he parked, it would be a simple matter of …

But don't overthink it, he cautioned himself.

The deed would be much more satisfying if it included a touch of spontaneity.

CHAPTER TWENTY NINE

Carly tried not to flinch when Lyle said gruffly, "I think it's time you explained something to me." He was driving them toward the edge of town in search of a place that Sierra Smith had told them about.

"What?" Carly replied, mentally sorting through things she could or could not explain to Lyle.

"Can you explain why we're going to a foundry?"

Carly drew a sigh of relief. She was already aware from her partner's face and his tone of voice that he was dubious about this trip. She couldn't blame him for his skepticism. She appreciated that he was giving her the benefit of the doubt—at least for now.

But she couldn't tell him the source of her sense of urgency—the dream vision she'd had of a woman's face filling up with what appeared to be blazing hot metal. When Sierra, the gallery owner, had mentioned foundries a few minutes ago, it had triggered Carly's hunch that the murderer might be working out of a foundry. She'd asked Sierra whether there were any foundries in the area, and Sierra had given them directions to one where area artists worked.

They were on their way there right now.

But Carly had to find something other than visionary dreams to make sense of it to Lyle. Fortunately, she did have other reasons to support her gut feeling.

She said to Lyle, "I've been thinking about the victims' faces, scrubbed clean and shaven, with no eyebrows and the hairline cut bare way up high on the head. There must be some reason. Then I remembered my art teacher in high school doing something that might explain all that."

"A high school teacher shaved off your hair?"

"Of course not. But she pulled our hair back tight and greased up our skin to make plaster molds of our faces. Then we used the mold to cast our own image in some other material. I think I made mine in some kind of purple stuff."

"Huh. Reminds me of death masks. Back before photography they made them so relatives could identify the dead."

"A lot of death masks were made of famous people—Napoleon,

Beethoven, even Nikola Tesla," Carly told him. "But you don't actually have to be dead. In class, we could breathe through straws while the casting plaster was poured on our faces."

She shuddered a little as she remembered that feeling of suffocation she'd gotten in the morgue.

"Maybe these women's faces were used to make plaster molds," she said. "But they didn't have straws to breathe through."

Lyle sputtered, "So you're saying—what? That the hairline and eyebrows were shaved to make plaster molds?"

"Right. And the faces were scrubbed clean afterwards to get rid of any hint of remaining grease or plaster."

"But why? Are you saying he's casting death masks?"

"Maybe he is. We seem to be dealing with a killer who feels a strong connection to Degas. Since Degas made images of the objects of his contempt, this guy might be doing something like that. The sight of those bronze reproductions of Degas's figures made me wonder if the killer wasn't casting the faces in bronze. If so, he'd need to do his work in some kind of a foundry."

"I don't know, Carly," Lyle said with a shake of his head. "You're making quite a few logical leaps here. It's pretty thin, as theories go."

Carly stifled a sigh.

I know how it sounds, she wanted to admit to Lyle. But she couldn't tell her partner about the visions of hot metal that shaped her own thinking.

Then Lyle added, "But I guess it's all we've got to go on. I just hope we're on the right track."

I hope so too, Carly thought as a sign came into view.

1/2 mile ahead
The Teapa Sculpture Center and Foundry

Maybe we'll catch a killer right there, she thought.

*

Nancy Ruhl felt a special spring in her step as she strode out of the late morning sunlight into the dimly lit parking garage. She was carrying a box containing a pair of new running shoes that she looked forward to breaking in.

I'm a woman of simple means, she thought with self-satisfaction as she jogged her way up the side stairs to the second level.

Back at the shoe store, she'd watched and listened as other women fretted aloud to each other over expensive footwear—perfectly useless shoes Nancy wouldn't be caught dead wearing.

How can anybody live that way? she wondered.

Sometimes it seemed like she was the only sane person in a perfectly crazy world.

She exited the stairwell into the parking level and listened to her own footsteps echo softly all around her. Her parked Honda scooter quickly came into view—another possession that marked her as a woman with healthy priorities. The scooter could reach a speed of 50 miles per hour and got 105 miles for every gallon of gas. What did Nancy need of anything bigger or faster?

She slowed her jogging to a halt as she arrived at the scooter. She put the box inside the seat compartment, put on her helmet, climbed onto the seat, and released the kickstand with a kick. But as she started her engine, she felt a telltale sag.

That had better not be what I think it is, she thought.

She turned off the engine, kicked the kickstand back into place, and got off the scooter and squeezed the back tire—which was completely empty of air.

She muttered a curse word under her breath, which echoed like a choir through the garage.

How did this happen? she thought.

She always did an excellent job of maintaining her vehicle, and she'd changed the tires less than a year ago.

Well, there's only one thing to do, Nancy thought.

She raised the scooter up on its center stand, then snapped open her seat compartment again and took out her tool kit.

Before she could get to work, she heard an echoing sound of someone whistling on the same parking level.

Whoever you are, just leave me alone, she thought, suppressing a growl.

Changing a tire was the sort of task she handled better unaided.

But as she heard the whistling coming closer, accompanied by footsteps. Then she heard a man's voice echoing nearby.

"Hey, do you need some help with that?"

She didn't turn to look at the man, who was now standing right behind her to her right. She just continued to use a ratchet wrench to loosen the spare tire attached behind the steering column below the handlebars.

"No, I'm good," she said.

"Are you sure? It's kind of a tough task for such a little lady."

Nancy bristled at those words.

He's got some nerve, she thought.

To make things worse, his voice sounded familiar. She was sure he'd said something obnoxious to her at one time or another recently. She couldn't quite place when or where.

She asked him curtly, "Have you ever changed a scooter tire?"

"No, but I've changed a car tire. This must be a lot easier."

"It's not," Nancy said, starting to disconnect the exhaust pipe in order to get at the flat tire. "It's actually harder. But I know what I'm doing, OK? If you try to help, you'll just get in the way. Just let me handle it."

"Well, there's no need to get defensive," the man said in a hurt voice.

And there's no need to get patronizing, she thought.

If this guy didn't go away, Nancy worried that she was going to have a hard time focusing on the task at hand—which really was more complicated than changing a car tire. She took off her helmet and shook her hair loose.

"Hey, you look a lot prettier without your helmet," the man said with a condescending chuckle.

This just gets worse and worse, Nancy thought.

And again, she thought the voice sounded familiar.

"Wait a minute," the man said. "I know you. Your name is Nancy."

Nancy paused from loosening a bolt and looked up at him. The guy looked pretty weird, wearing a hat with earflaps down and his jacket collar turned up on what was actually warm, pleasant morning. More outlandish still, he was wearing mirrored sunglasses in this dimly lit place.

I guess he thinks he looks cool like that, he thought.

Like some kind of spy.

She felt like telling him he looked geeky instead of cool—and not geeky in a good way.

He snapped his fingers and said, "Yeah, we were in the same drawing class together, just a few days ago."

Nancy's lips curled with annoyance as she finally recognized the guy. He'd come up behind her in a still-life class and had told her that her drawing was "pretty." She wouldn't have taken offense, except that she knew her drawing was actually quite crude. She wished she could draw, but no matter how many classes she took, she just never got the hang of it.

They guy had obviously meant to hit on her, but she'd managed to fend him off by glaring at him and then simply ignoring him.

This time, simply ignoring him was not an option.

"Nice to see you again," she grumbled. "Now let me get back to work."

But as she turned her attention back to the tire, she saw something she hadn't noticed before.

There was a small, sharp, clean slash in the tire.

Someone had done this deliberately with some sort of blade.

This guy, maybe?

She felt a creeping fear that he might not be as harmless as he seemed.

Her mind flashed through a repertoire of self-defense techniques she'd learned over the years. The simplest, of course, was pepper spray, which she kept in her handbag.

But before she could reach for it, the man grabbed her from behind, slapping a wet cloth over her mouth and nose.

This taste, she thought.

This smell.

She didn't know what the sticky liquid was, but she did know she was in terrible danger. But before her combative reflexes kicked in, she heard what sounded like white noise, and her field of vision filled up with a blizzard of sparkling light.

Then everything was gone.

CHAPTER THIRTY

As their vehicle neared the Teapa Sculpture Center and Foundry, Carly heard Lyle's phone buzz. Since Lyle was driving, he pulled out his phone and handed it to her.

"Would you check that for me?"

Carly suppressed a discouraged sigh when she looked at the caller's I.D.

"It's a text message from Sheriff Ketchum."

"Naturally. What's he want?"

Carly read the message aloud.

Where are you guys? What are you doing now?

Lyle let out a slight scoff and said, "Good questions, I guess."

"What should I text him?"

"Tell him we're following a lead. Say we'll report back soon."

As Carly typed the reply and sent it, she was thinking, *I sure hope we'll have something to report.*

A message came back from the sheriff:

Work fast. We need to compare notes ASAP.

Lyle let out a harsh laugh when she read it to him. "That means he's getting nowhere. He's hoping we can give him something to go on."

I sure hope so too, Carly thought as she texted a final "OK" to the sheriff.

Lyle parked their car and they got out. The morning air was fresh, and the scene was quite attractive. The area in front of a group of brick buildings had been turned into an outdoor sculpture gallery. On their way toward what appeared to be the main entrance, they walked past bronze images of a life-sized jungle cat, a powerful-looking robed woman, and a large abstract form that turned in response to the slightest breeze. Other sculptures were in view among an array of small gardens.

"It doesn't look very ominous," Lyle said. Then he quickly added, "Of course, the same thing might have been said about Cottage Grove

Park this morning, except for the corpse in the gazebo."

Carly nodded. She knew that even a peaceful place like this might harbor a psychopathic killer.

Just outside the main building, three boys were playing with a Frisbee. One who had a shock of pale blonde hair appeared to be in his late teens, while two with darker hair and skin tones were somewhat younger.

Lyle held out his badge and said to the boys, "Sorry to interrupt your game. We're from the FBI, and we need to talk to whoever is in charge here."

One of the younger boys caught the Frisbee, and the oldest stepped toward Lyle for a closer look at his badge.

"Wow," he said. "Feds, huh? This must be something serious."

The boy opened the front door and called inside, "Hey, Dad, you'd better come out here. A couple of FBI agent are here on a visit."

A few seconds later, a man stepped out of the building. He was a sturdy, brown-skinned man with a dark beard and thick black hair. He was wearing overalls and had a set of goggles hanging around his neck. He pulled off a pair of work gloves as he walked toward them.

"Care to show me some badges?" he asked Carly and Lyle.

Carly and Lyle took out their badges and introduced themselves.

"Special agents?" the man said. "Well, you must have the wrong address, I reckon. There's nothing illegal going on here."

Carly explained, "We're investigating a group of murders."

The man's eyes widened. "You mean that woman a couple of days ago?" he asked. "And I heard there was another death this morning."

"That's right," Lyle replied, staring stone-faced at him.

Shaking his head, the man replied, "Well, I can't imagine how we can help. But if you've got reason to think otherwise, we'll do our best. Teapa is a peaceful town—or at least it was until a couple of days ago. We liked it that way. And we'd like to get things back to normal."

The man offered a rough, strong hand for Carly and Lyle to shake.

"My name's Martín Gutiérez, and these are my boys, Bruno, Diego, and Luis. Come on inside and I'll introduce you to … heh … the little lady."

Carly noticed an unmistakable note of irony in how he said those words, "little lady."

Carly and Lyle followed him through a front foyer, then into a startlingly large, hot, and noisy area that looked almost like a small factory.

Except there's no assembly line, Carly thought.

Instead, there were a number of people at work on an array of sculptures in various stages of completion.

She wondered, *Is this the place I dreamed about last night?*

She was sure that one of the victims had tried to show her the killer's lair, but little about that vision had come into focus. She had glimpsed a long table scattered with lumps of clay, with coiled wire hanging above it.

She didn't see anything like that here.

Carly struggled to recall any other images she might have seen.

Nothing.

But she did remember one thing clearly.

It was dark there.

Dimly lit.

And it felt ...

The only word she could think of was *confined.* The place in her dream had been closed off in some way.

This big bright, cheerful, bustling space didn't resemble it at all.

Carly's heart sank at the possibility that she'd brought them to the wrong place. She was sure that the killer intended to murder seven women, to complete the Degas sequence of seven dance positions. He'd only taken three so far.

They didn't have any time to waste on dead ends.

But surely, she thought, *somebody here knows something that can help us.*

Martín Gutiérez led Carly and Lyle over to a large, abstract bronze sculpture, where a pair of women wearing face shields and fire-resistant suits were at work. The larger of them held a welding torch.

Martín touched the larger woman on the shoulder and spoke loudly enough for her to hear over the roar of the torch.

"Hey, Robin—we've got official company."

The woman turned off the torch and lifted up the face shield to reveal a wide, ruddy face. Carly could tell at a glance she was not only big but as tough as nails. She felt willing to bet that this woman was very good at all that she did.

"Little lady," indeed, Carly thought with a slight smile.

Martín introduced them, "This is my wife, Robin, and my daughter Debbie. As you can see, they're pretty much in charge of the welding here."

He told his wife, "These are FBI agents investigating the murders."

"Oh, my goodness!" Robin said with a gasp. She pulled off her headgear, revealing blond hair tied tightly back. "Is there anything we can do to help catch this killer?"

"That's what we're here to find out," Lyle said. "We have reason to suspect that he's a local sculptor."

Debbie also removed her headgear. "That just can't be true," she stated firmly.

Meanwhile, the three Gutiérez boys had quit their Frisbee game and had come inside. They joined the group to gawk, but they listened quietly.

Carly saw that the daughter, like two of the boys, looked very much like their father. The older boy more closely resembled his mother. She wondered if they all lived right here at the foundry.

"Oh, I can't believe that," Robin sputtered. "The art community here in Teapa is really tight and close-knit, like a big extended family. Martín and I do business with all the sculptors in town—at least the ones who do metal work. They're all good people."

Debbie added, "I'm sure there's not a one of them capable of murder."

Although the two women sounded convinced of this, Carly knew that people typically didn't like to think ill of those they knew and worked with.

"Do a lot of artists live here at the foundry?" she asked.

"Some do," Robin answered. "There's a nice row of homes back away from these work buildings. We share a community kitchen, but we all have our separate living quarters."

"And we have gardens," Debbie said. "We raise a lot of our own food."

"Artists who don't live here bring pieces to us for casting," Robin explained. "That's a good part of our income."

"What makes you think the killer's a sculptor?" Martín put in.

"He apparently makes something like death masks of his victims," Lyle said.

Robin shrugged and said, "That's not necessarily a work of art."

"But maybe they could be," Carly ventured. "We think he might cast them in bronze."

At least that's my hunch, she thought.

Of course, her dream was her real reason for thinking such a thing.

"No," Robin said with an anxious shake of her head. "No, I don't believe that."

Lyle said to Robin, "You just said local sculptors bring their work here to be cast in bronze."

"That's right," the woman replied.

"Have you cast any mask-like bronze pieces lately?" Lyle asked.

"No, I'm pretty sure we haven't," Martín put in. "I'd remember something like that."

"So would I," Robin said.

Debbie just shook her head.

"Is there any way to check for certain?" Lyle asked.

"Sure," Robin told him. "Come with me."

Robin said to her daughter, "You just keep working, hon."

Debbie nodded and began to put her headgear back on.

The three boys followed their parents and Carly and Lyle into a nearby office.

Martín walked over to a desk scattered with record books. Although there was a small computer on a corner of the desk, Carly could see that Martín kept his records the old-fashioned way, with pen and ink.

Probably a good thing, Carly thought, remembering a few times that she'd lost computer files. In her experience, ink and paper were sometimes more reliable.

Martín thumbed through a huge ledger that lay open on the desk for a few moments. Then he shook his head.

"Nope," he said. "Everything we do is in this book, and there's nothing like that here."

Lyle asked, "And nobody could have done pieces like that on the sly?"

Martín and Robin both chuckled.

Robin said, "It's kind of tough to cast anything in bronze 'on the sly.' The whole thing is a pretty involved process."

"What about when you're closed for the night?" Carly asked.

"We've got somebody watching the place around the clock," Martín said. "Besides that, somebody can be working at any hour."

"And we live here," the oldest boy muttered. "People are all over this place all the time."

Lyle scratched his chin and thought for a moment.

Then he said, "Suppose it wasn't an order on the books. Couldn't one of your employers have done something like that without anybody noticing?"

Robin chuckled some more.

"I'm afraid you're barking up the wrong tree, Agent Ramsey. This place is run like a collective. All the employees own part of it, and they share in the profits. We all know what's being worked on."

Martín put in, "There isn't anyone in this building we haven't known for years, some of them since they were kids."

"Some of them since *we* were kids," Robin added.

Lyle asked, "And none of them have been behaving strangely?"

"No, and we'd know about that, for sure," Martín said.

The oldest boy added with a laugh, "Actually, *everybody* here would know about it. This place is a regular gossip mill. There's not much privacy here."

One of the younger boys grumbled, "Makes me crazy sometimes."

Carly and Lyle exchanged a look. Carly was certain that she and her partner were thinking the same thing.

There's nothing sinister going on here.

Then Lyle said, "Maybe you could talk us through the whole casting process."

"We'd be glad to," Martín said. "Follow me."

Carly and Lyle followed Martín and Robin and their boys into an area where a number of sculptures were being prepared for the process. A couple of employees were pouring a thick white liquid over one of the forms.

Robin said, "We use wax sculptures as part of the process of casting bronze sculptures. Sometimes we get the artist's original already in wax, and then we can go straight to the final steps. But most often when we get it here, it has been made in a type of modeling clay, which is easier to work and supports a lot of detail. So we have to get the clay sculpture into wax and then to bronze. First, we make a negative image, a mold, from the clay original."

They continued over to another area, where hot, melted wax was being poured into one of the hollow forms.

Robin explained, "We use that mold to make a wax replica of the original sculpture. Then the artist can either work on that or rely on us to touch it up for them. When it's ready, we make another mold directly over the wax, then melt the wax right out of it. Because wax can be burned away completely, our new mold is very accurate. We use that one to cast the final bronze. As it happens, you're in luck—we're going to cast something right now."

As Robin led them into a new work area, they could feel a blast of heat.

"Stand back here," she told them firmly. "You're not dressed for this."

As they watched, two men wearing protective clothing used long-handled tongs to draw a large, bucket-shaped container out of a fiery furnace. The container was supported by a chain on an overhead track.

"That container is called a crucible," Robin said. "It contains the molten bronze that will get shaped into a sculpture."

The two men guided the crucible to a nearby mold. They tilted the crucible, and lava-like liquid came pouring out, making a violent hissing sound as it made its way inside the mold.

Carly felt overwhelmed by the sight.

That hot hissing noise, she remembered from her most recent dream.

The flowing hot metal.

She knew the killer had followed this process. But instead of beginning with clay or wax, he made molds of the dead women's faces.

He created a bronze death mask from each victim's face.

But she felt equally certain that it hadn't happened here.

Suddenly she felt a presence—the same spirit, she thought, who had come to her in her most recent dream.

She saw the hot metal assuming a distinct shape.

It was the fiery, eyeless face she'd seen in her dream.

Its lips moved as it spoke in a voice that only Carly could hear.

"He has taken somebody else. Another woman is about to die."

CHAPTER THIRTY ONE

Don't lose control, Carly commanded herself.

In her internal vision, the hot, glowing, eyeless mask still hovered there in front of her. Its lips were moving again.

"He has taken somebody else," the mask repeated.

Carly struggled to grasp the meaning of those terrible words without visibly reacting to them. She couldn't let the intensity of this contact overwhelm her now, not in front of Lyle and the Gutiérez family and everybody else at work here in the foundry.

But then she heard the mask speak yet again.

"Do you hear me? Another woman is about to die."

The spirit sounded impatient now—and Carly could imagine why. While she and Lyle and the local cops had been struggling to close this case, the killer had captured another woman. And now the spirit of one of his previous victims expected Carly to stop him before he killed yet again.

Of course, Carly couldn't answer aloud. Nevertheless, she did all she could to send a mental response.

I hear you.

I really do hear you.

The vision of the glowing mask faded, and her view returned to solid, ordinary physical reality. She found herself looking again at the stream of metal being poured into the mold.

And still she heard a final murmured question from the spirit, *"What are you going to do about it?"*

Carly felt weak at her knees now.

She knew she couldn't lie—not to the spirit of a murder victim.

Again, she replied with her thoughts.

We're doing all we can.

The voice replied with a sigh of despair.

"That's not good enough."

Then the presence waned, and the world turned normal again …

If normal is the right word for it.

She saw that Lyle had been watching the pouring of the bronze with wide-eyed interest.

"Wow, that's really amazing," he said to the Gutiérez family. "Almost magical. But how do you …?"

His voice faded, but Martín Gutiérez completed his question with a chuckle.

"Release the sculpture from the cast? Come over here and we'll show you."

The grouped walked over to another area, where a couple of workmen were cracking open a cocooned sculpture. A bronze, bigger-than-life Native American warrior was starting to emerge.

Robin was explaining the last phases of the process, including the use of the welding torch to correct details and the application of a surface coating called the patina.

But Carly wasn't really listening.

That voice kept echoing through her head.

"He has taken somebody else."

Carly didn't doubt for a second that the spirit was telling the truth.

She also recognized the truth of the other comment.

"That's not good enough."

And now she was also absolutely sure of something else.

The victim isn't in this foundry.

Nobody who works here took her.

Finally, Carly broke into the conversation.

"Are there any other foundries in this area?" she asked the Gutiérez family.

Martín shook his head and said, "No, there's just us. Not many local artists do this kind of work anymore."

The older boy with the shock of pale blonde hair spoke up.

"Actually, that's not quite true, Dad. There's also Apollo Iron and Steel."

Martín scoffed slightly and said, "Yeah, but that's been closed up for ages."

"Folks say it's haunted," said the youngest son.

"There's no such thing as ghosts," his mother said with a wag of her finger.

"Maybe not," said the middle son, "but I've also heard there have been lights over there at night lately."

"So have I," the oldest son said.

"That's just talk," Martín scoffed.

"No, it's not, Dad," the daughter said. "I saw lights there a couple of nights ago when I drove by the place."

Carly and Lyle exchanged an interested look.

"What can you tell us about this foundry?" Lyle asked.

Martín shrugged and said, "It was more like a factory, really. It served as both a steel mill and a foundry, and also a place where equipment got manufactured. Back in the late 1800s, during the heyday of railroad construction here in New Mexico, there was a huge need for iron and steel for all kinds of equipment—especially rails. That's when the factory got built. Of course, railroad construction declined over the years, and so did the need for steel. So Apollo Iron and Steel closed down … how long ago was that, Robin?"

Martín's wife squinted with thought and said, "Sometime in the middle of the 20th century, I guess. It's just a big, sprawled-out ruin now."

The youngest son repeated, "Folks say it's haunted."

Martín ruffled the boy's hair and said, "No, it's not, son."

The middle son said, "But Debbie says she saw lights out there."

The daughter nodded and said, "That's right. I actually saw them more than once when I drove by there at night." She frowned at her brothers and added, "I didn't say it was ghosts, though."

"Probably squatters," Martín said.

"Yeah, probably," his wife added.

Carly could tell by Lyle's expression that his curiosity was piqued, as was hers.

"Could you tell my partner and I how to get there?" Lyle asked. "In case it doesn't come up on GPS?"

"Sure," Martín said, sounding a little surprised by Lyle's interest. "It's about 20 miles west of here."

Martín offered some directions and Lyle jotted them down. He and Carly thanked the family for their time and help, then headed out of the foundry.

As they got into their vehicle, Lyle said, "I guess it's kind of a long shot, but lights at night mean *somebody's* there. I say we drive on over there and have a look for ourselves."

Carly nodded in agreement. She thought the same thing. The brightly lit foundry they had just left hadn't matched the images she'd gotten of some dark, gloomy interior. An abandoned factory certainly sounded more likely.

But it was twenty miles away, and the spirit's words were still rattling through her brain.

"Another woman is about to die."

As Lyle drove toward their destination, she kept hearing the spirit's accusation.

"That's not good enough."

She was beset by worries that bordered on panic.

There wasn't a spare minute for making mistakes. Suppose she and Lyle were wrong in their hunch about the factory? What if they were going to the wrong place?

But what else have we got to go on? she wondered.

She felt a mounting frustration about the messages she received. There seemed to be more of them now and from different spirits. They were becoming more powerful over time, and more insistent. But she lacked control over who she could contact and what she could learn.

Would her gift soon become unmanageable?

Is it unmanageable already?

They were now driving across the open desert, and Carly saw nothing up ahead that gave her any hope of soon reaching their destination.

In the meantime, Lyle was talking aloud.

"The whole thing is making more sense by the minute. I think I'm even getting a profile of the killer. He's a misogynist, of course. But a guy who grows up with that kind of hatred of women has a problem with men as well ..."

Carly found it hard to listen to what Lyle was saying. She felt desperate to tell him what she knew—or what she thought she knew. But what could she say? She couldn't very well tell him she'd just gotten a message from a murder victim telling her that another woman had been abducted.

Lyle kept talking while she worried.

"From his childhood on, he never once felt accepted by males his age, never bonded with them, never felt like 'one of the boys.' He's never experienced any kind of comradeship. He's desperately lonely ..."

Finally, Carly couldn't keep silent any longer.

"Lyle, I think maybe you should drive faster," she said, interrupting him.

"Faster? Why?"

Carly struggled for a moment to find the right words.

But there really weren't any.

Instead she simply blurted out, "I think he's already abducted another victim."

Lyle's eyes widened as he glanced over at her.

"You *think* so?" he asked.

"Yes."

"Why do you think so?"

Carly felt truly stymied now.

But I've got to tell him something, she thought.

Finally, she said, "I've got a really, really, really strong feeling."

Lyle glanced at her again.

"You get these feelings a lot, don't you?"

More and more all the time, she thought.

But she nodded silently instead of saying so aloud.

Lyle's expression struck Carly as more curious than skeptical. And he also looked worried.

Finally, he said, "Well, I guess we'd better hurry then."

He pressed the accelerator harder, and the car moved faster along the desert road. Finally a large, dark building came into view.

"There's the old factory," Lyle said.

Carly's spirits sank at the sight. It seemed ominous and intimidating.

And huge, she thought.

It looked like an old fortress, with connected buildings stretching in all directions. As Martín and his family had said, it was a decrepit ruin. Windows were broken everywhere, and Carly could even see places where the roof had collapsed.

In the late afternoon daylight, they could see no lights glowing through the darkness inside the structure.

If the killer and his next victim were in there, how hard was it going to be for her and Lyle to find them?

"Maybe we should call Ketchum for some help," Carly said.

"Maybe. But I doubt he'll want to spare any of his cops. He'll want more than our hunches before he'll do that."

As if in reply, Lyle's phone rang.

Carly felt a surge of dread at the sound.

I know who that is, she thought.

I know what he's going to say.

CHAPTER THIRTY TWO

"You'd better answer it," Lyle said, passing his phone to Carly.

Her fingers shook as she took it. When she heard Sheriff Ketchum's voice, she again felt certain about what he was going to say. She put the call on speakerphone so both she and Lyle could communicate with him.

Ketchum sounded anxious.

"We need your help. There's been a new development."

"What's that?" Lye asked.

"We think there's been another abduction."

Lyle's mouth dropped open as he glanced sideways at Carly.

His expression seemed to say, *"You knew!"*

Ketchum sounded increasingly agitated as he continued.

"We can't be positive. But somebody found an abandoned motor scooter in a parking garage in town. The back tire was slashed, and it looks like whoever owned the scooter had been in the middle of changing the tire. But the owner was nowhere in sight."

Lyle asked calmly, "Are you sure the owner didn't just go for help?"

"We thought that at first. But a shoebox was dropped right there with a brand-new pair of sneakers spilling out. And it turns out the owner is a young woman, similar to the earlier victims. Of course, we can't be *absolutely* sure this has anything to do with our killer, but ..."

Ketchum's voice faded. His silence told Carly that he was pretty sure of the worst.

And she was too.

"Where are the two of you, anyway?" Ketchum asked. "We need to get together and on the same page ASAP."

Lyle squinted and his face twitched. Carly could tell he was going to make a big decision.

"Sheriff, my partner and I are out at Apollo Iron and Steel."

"The abandoned factory?" Ketchum asked with an incredulous gasp. "What the hell are you doing all the way out there?"

"We've got reason to think that's where the killer is," Lyle replied. "Hiding out in this old factory. And there's a good chance he's holding the victim in there with him."

If he hasn't killed her already, Carly thought.

But no spirit's voice had let her know that the woman was dead. So there was a chance they were here in time.

Lyle continued to the sheriff, "It looks like a big place. The two of us are going to enter and search, and we need for you to send backup."

"You really think he's in there?"

"Yes, we do. There's no time to explain."

"You'll hold off until we get there?"

"No. We're going in now."

"OK, I'll send backup," Sheriff Ketchum said.

Lyle ended the call and Carly handed back his phone.

"You're right," she told him. "We have to hurry."

As he opened his car door, he gave her another sideways glance.

"Let's go, then," he said.

Carly scrambled out of the car, and they stood together staring at the complex of buildings on the far side of a tall, gated fence. She felt her confidence sag.

"It looks like a huge maze," she said. "How are the two of us going to even start hunting him?"

Lyle pointed out to two separate doorways, "It looks like those are the main ways in. I'll go in the one to the right, you go in to the left. We need to find out if he's actually in there and if he's holding another woman. But if either of us finds anything, hears anything, or even suspects anything, we call the other. Our phones should just be on vibrate."

As they adjusted their phones, Lyle added firmly, "Take no action until we're both ready. If we can, we'll wait for backup to arrive."

"OK."

Taking his own weapon out of his holster, Lyle added, "And have your Glock ready. You're liable to need it. And your flashlight too."

With that, they both headed toward the fence in front of the building.

*

The bound girl didn't move or make a sound as Derek Kuchan smeared oil on her face. She didn't even flinch as his fingers spread the liquid under the blindfold.

Still out cold from the chloroform, he realized.

The other three women had started to come out of it by this stage in his process. Of course, he could carry out his task while she was still unconscious, but that would be most unsatisfying.

He slapped the face gently and said in a purring voice, "Wake up, my dear."

The woman moaned almost inaudibly.

He had the electric razor ready to shave her scalp and eyebrows, and a bucket of thick plaster to pour over her face. He held the hypodermic full of vecuronium at the ready, waiting for just the right moment to inject it into the artery in the crook of her outstretched arm.

But he just bent over her with the syringe in his hand, watching for signs of awareness.

He wanted her to hear him lie to her, just as he had to the others:

"This will hurt only for a moment."

He wanted her to be fully awake and aware of her own creeping paralysis and impending suffocation.

But the woman remained in a profound stupor. She seemed to be even weaker than the others. Her sluggishness filled him with disgust, and he had to restrain himself from simply killing her right now.

Then Derek heard an ominous sound from just outside.

With a jolt of alarm, he jerked upright and listened.

Someone's coming through the front gate.

Was it just some unsuspecting trespasser or had the police discovered his lair?

With the hypodermic still in his hand, Derek left the enormous hall that was his lair and crept down a short hallway toward the entrance.

He peered out through a broken window.

A man was approaching the building—an African American man with a weapon drawn. He would soon be inside.

It's the police, all right, he realized.

Even so, Derek felt unexpectedly calm about this new development. For one thing, the cop seemed to be unaccompanied. For another thing . . .

He tapped a finger against the hypodermic syringe.

I know just what to do, he thought with a smile.

*

With her Glock drawn, Carly hurried along toward a large pair of double doors. She and Lyle had parted ways as soon as they got through the old gate, and she knew he had headed toward a different entrance. She glanced back but couldn't see where he was now.

She reached the doors and tentatively turned the knob on one. To her surprise, it swung open without any trouble.

Carly stepped inside. She found herself in a wide hallway with a high ceiling. Several tall broken windows spread the fading sunlight across a linoleum-tiled floor. It was very quiet. Even her own footsteps sounded loud as she turned and looked around.

The place seemed even more vast from the inside than it had outside. No signs indicated what she might find in any direction.

She moved forward, trying to keep her tread quiet, but the space acted almost like an amplifier for the sound of every step she took.

So much for the element of surprise, she thought.

She randomly decided to take a hallway that led off to the left. The light was just a dim glow shining through doors that opened into empty rooms, and also from a rupture in the building's roof. She still saw no sign that anyone else was in the building.

Suddenly an odd sound caught her attention. It was as though she could hear the echo of her own footsteps.

Carly stopped walking and stood still, listening.

The sound of footsteps continued a few beats and then stopped.

Someone else's footsteps, she realized.

Someone else was here and apparently aware of her presence.

She felt her heart beating faster.

Then she remembered what Lyle had said.

"If either of us finds anything, hears anything, or even suspects anything, we call the other."

But Carly was too focused on listening for those sounds to pull out her phone and call Lyle. Sure enough, the footsteps soon resumed. She couldn't see anyone, but she felt sure she must be hearing the killer somewhere in the dimly lit old building.

I can't let him get away, she thought.

But she couldn't tell which direction the noise came from, nor from how far away. Her gun still drawn, she moved slowly in what she hoped was the right direction. A short distance up ahead, another hallway branched off to the right.

She heard the footsteps stop, and then the bumping sound of a door closing.

Carly slowed her breathing to stay calm.

She moved up to the branching hallway and saw where it led—

which was hardly anywhere. It was a short dead-end passageway with several closed doors. Everything was suddenly silent. She knew her target must have stepped through one of those doors. Was he still somewhere in this cul-de-sac, or had he found an exit from the building?

She called out in an endlessly echoing voice.

"This is the FBI. Come out with your hands up."

Silence fell again.

Carly began to move down the dim, windowless hallway, wondering which door might be concealing the killer. She pulled out her flashlight and turned it on.

And how can I find out?

Then she heard a loud noise, as if an object had been knocked over, followed by a groan of despair. Carly spotted the source of the noise. It had come from behind a door marked MAINTENANCE.

She stepped toward the door and called out again.

"Come out with your hands out."

There was no reply. Again, Carly considered calling Lyle. But Carly had no doubt that she had her target securely trapped. She could take him into custody right now.

She reached for the doorknob and turned it.

The door opened to reveal a young woman crouched on the floor, her hands raised and her eyes wide with terror. Tears were pouring down her face.

Her eyes widened when she saw Carly.

"Are you really FBI?" the woman cried out with a sob.

CHAPTER THIRTY THREE

Carly could hardly believe her eyes. A trembling, weeping woman was staring wildly at her, here in a maintenance closet of the dilapidated building.

This has to be the new victim, she thought as she holstered her gun. But the sheriff hadn't given them many details about her.

She kept her flashlight on because it was the only light in this dark room.

"How did you get here?" Carly asked.

"I escaped. From … from a monster."

Carly felt a chill. That surely meant that she and Lyle had come to the right place.

"He doesn't have you now," Carly told her. "What's your name?"

"Nancy Ruhl."

"And you were kidnapped?"

"He knocked me out somehow in a parking garage, and then I woke up somewhere else. Strapped to a table. With my eyes blindfolded."

"How did you get loose?"

Nancy gasped breathlessly, holding up a wrist with a leather strap hanging from it.

"He was smearing something greasy all over my face, but I didn't let him know I was awake. I realized that this strap had come loose from the table, but I played possum, waiting for some kind of chance."

She giggled a little hysterically as she continued, "Then I heard him walking away. I used my free hand to pull off my blindfold. He was gone."

She looked wildly around the little room, as though she expected him to appear.

"I grabbed my chance to unbuckle the other straps. Then I just ran like hell. I didn't know where I was going, but I didn't know what else to do."

Carly felt a swell of admiration for Nancy Ruhl.

"You did fine," she said. "You did just fine. I take it you haven't seen your attacker since you got loose."

The woman shook her head.

"Do you know where he is?"

The woman shook her head again.

He could be anywhere, Carly thought.

It was definitely time to get in touch with Lyle. She took out her cellphone and punched in his number.

*

Lyle was only dimly aware of his phone vibrating in his pocket. He had just walked into a gigantic manufacturing hall that was illuminated—however dimly—with dozens of small electric lamps. The huge windows were covered over with cardboard.

At the far end of the hall, Lyle saw a huge, mighty crucible that had once been used to pour tons of molten steel. But what most astonished him was a row of seven life-sized statues of women in what appeared to be dancing poses. And they were all too familiar.

The Degas dancers, he realized.

He could feel his skin crawl as he saw that three of the figures had bronze mask-like faces. The other four faces were blank, with no features at all.

Nearby was a blazing furnace with a much smaller crucible in it. The crucible was bubbling and glowing with liquid bronze.

Closer to him and off to one side was a metal table rigged with unbuckled leather straps,

The killer's lair, Lyle realized.

His phone vibrated again, and this time Lyle was fully aware of it. But before he could reach for it, he was struck from behind.

He felt a sharp jab in the side of his neck.

Suddenly his whole body felt like rubber.

His gun flew out of his hand, and he collapsed to the floor.

As Lyle struggled to regain some muscular control, he realized that someone was standing in front of him. He looked up to see a smiling man holding a hypodermic needle.

Lyle realized what he'd been stabbed with.

He murmured aloud, "Vecuronium."

The man chuckled and said, "Very good, sir. You know your paralytic drugs, I see." He looked at the syringe in his hand. "You didn't get much, and it works best when injected directly into an artery. The opportunity didn't present itself with you. But judging from your present condition, it's still working reasonably well."

The man casually tossed the hypodermic away.

But then he gasped with alarm.

Pointing to the empty table at the side of the room, he said, "But where is she?"

He grabbed Lyle by the back of his collar and shouted, "Tell me where she is!"

"I don't know who you mean."

The man's smile slowly returned, and he said in a calmer voice, "Of course you don't know. How stupid of me. You just got here yourself. Is anybody with you?"

"No," Lyle lied.

"Why should I believe you?"

"Don't believe me if you don't want to."

He was groping around now, managing to hoist himself up onto his elbows.

The man said, "Looking for this?"

He held Lyle's pistol in front of him.

Lyle couldn't suppress a groan of despair.

"Damn it," he muttered.

It was the first time he could remember ever losing control of his weapon.

The man pointed the gun in Lyle's face and said, "As it happens, I do know how to use one of these."

Where's Carly? Lyle wondered.

He felt foolish for not reaching for his phone the second he'd felt it vibrate.

He was weakening more every second. The paralysis was progressing, and he knew he'd soon be beyond incapacitated. He'd be worse than helpless.

Keep him talking, he told himself.

Lyle struggled to hold his head up and look around. His own voice sounded far away to him.

"Your work … Degas poses, aren't they?"

The man tilted his head and crinkled his brow.

"As a matter of fact, they are," he said.

I've piqued his curiosity, Lyle thought. *But I've got to hold his interest.*

Studying the figures as well as he could, he said, "I see that you've made those pieces like Degas made his—wire and wax and clay and whatever else you could manage."

The man's smile flickered again.

Lyle managed to add, "It's very impressive."

The man looked positively intrigued now.

Flattery might keep me alive, Lyle thought.

He continued, "You plan to cast them in bronze."

"That's right."

Peering at the statues again, Lyle said, "I see you've already made bronze masks for three of them. Death masks of the murdered women, aren't they? And you're going to make four more. Wow, that's going to make some statement."

"Statement?" the man asked with mounting interest.

"Sure," Lyle said, struggling against the mounting paralysis. "Most people don't understand Degas. They don't know what he was really trying to say. But *you're* going to tell them. More power to you."

"You feel the same way about … ?" the man asked with surprise.

Lyle rallied his energy and replied, "Hell, do you have any idea what it's like working with women in law enforcement? The whole sex—the whole ape-like lot of them—they've gotten way too much power; they've gotten way out of control. But you … you're liable to change the whole damned world."

The man's eyes had widened now. He clearly didn't know what to say—or do.

Struggling to think, to keep talking, Lyle remembered something he'd said to Carly in the car.

"He's never experienced any kind of comradeship. He's desperately lonely."

His lips were getting numb, and he could hear a hissing sound in his voice as he forced out his words.

"Wonderful factory. But you'll need to use that big old crucible. Alone."

"I'll manage," the man croaked defensively.

"You're expecting an army of men … eager to help."

"That's right."

"Consider me your first recruit … *sir."*

Lyle could say no more. His voice was gone, and his limbs were going positively numb now.

He saw that the killer was wavering between credulity and disbelief.

Lyle's elbows gave out from under him, but he barely felt his face hit the floor.

Then he heard a sinister chuckle.

"Clever try," the man said. "But I'll never have a cop for a soldier. Never."

Then Lyle heard the sound of his gun being cocked.

CHAPTER THIRTY FOUR

Carly fought against panic as she ran through labyrinthine hallways.

Lyle hadn't answered his phone.

She had no idea where he was or what might have happened to him. But she knew from the woman she had found in the maintenance closet that the killer was here in one of these buildings.

And Lyle was somewhere in this maze too. She could only hope that Nancy Ruhl was leading her in the right direction.

Finally the two of them arrived at a pair of double doors.

"He was holding me in there," Nancy said as she reached for the doorknob.

"Wait," Carly hissed. "Don't open it. You need to stay right here. Don't move until I tell you it's OK."

The woman nodded and backed away from the door.

Carly took a deep breath. Then with her weapon at the ready, she opened the door and stepped into the room.

She gasped with horror at what she saw.

Her partner was sprawled on the floor of a gigantic factory room lit with electric lanterns and cluttered with weird objects. She also felt heat from a small, blazing furnace.

The room the spirit tried to show me, she thought.

A man standing over Lyle had a gun pointed at his head.

"Don't shoot!" Carly called out. "Put down your weapon and raise your hands."

The man turned his head to see Carly, but he didn't move his gun away from Lyle.

He smiled and said, "Try to stop me."

"If you kill him, you'll be the next to die," Carly cried, trying to sound threatening.

"Really?"

Without wavering his aim, the man moved around so that he could see her better. "Are you really capable of using deadly force?"

"Yes, I have."

And of course, it was true.

The man chuckled, "You're only a woman. Excuse me if I'm not scared."

For a moment Carly was swept with confusion. Although she'd rather just wound him, she was certainly willing to kill this man if that's what it came to. But shooting him probably wouldn't save Lyle's life. The killer's gun would likely go off if he was hit.

Now the man was peering at her with increasing interest, looking her up and down like some kind of leering pervert.

"Maybe we can work something out," he told her. "As a matter of fact, your arrival could be quite appropriate."

He looked her up and down again.

"A little older than the others. In the master's time, you'd be dead by now anyway, from the diseases of your own depravity. But you suit my purposes well enough. You can be my number four. And I'll catch up with the one who ran away. I know this building well, and she's not smart enough to escape me. I'd have her by now if you people hadn't interfered. She can be number five. That brings me much closer to my goal."

As he droned on, Carly realized what he meant. She herself bore a physical resemblance to the women he'd been abducting and killing.

He wants me to be his next victim.

The man continued, "Drop your weapon and do everything I say. Then I'll let your friend go. It'll be your life for his."

Lyle's life for mine.

A memory flashed through her mind.

She and Lyle had been talking together in a bar one night. Lyle, of course, had been drinking nothing but sparkling water, but Carly had gotten more than a little tipsy, and her tongue was wagging freely.

"I love you, Lyle. I don't mean romantically. I mean like a pal. A colleague. A comrade. A friend."

Lyle chuckled and said, "I know what you mean. I love you that way too."

Then Carly blurted, "I'd take a bullet for you."

"Oh, Carly ...," Lyle began with a smile and a shake of his head.

"You think I don't mean it?"

"Of course I think you mean it. I also know you're a little drunk. But let me tell you something—and I haven't touched a drink for years."

He took hold of Carly's hand and said to her quietly.

"I'd definitely take a bullet for you rather than see you shot."

The whole world and time itself seemed to slow down to a halt as the memory faded.

Lyle's life for mine, Carly thought again.

She started to lower her weapon; she heard an unfamiliar spirit voice speaking to her out of nowhere, out of thin air.

"Don't do this, Carly."

Carly suppressed a gasp of shock.

She replied silently, *"I've got to."*

"No. Even if Lyle goes free, he couldn't go on with life. It would kill him with guilt."

"There's no other way."

"Please. I can't help him anymore. It's up to you to be there for him ... always."

"Who are *you?"*

But before the spirit could reply, another voice rang out —the shouted voice of a living, flesh-and-blood woman.

"Hey, you!"

The man with the gun jerked around to look in the direction of the sound.

Nancy Ruhl stood there inside the door.

The killer's arm wavered as he seemed to be undecided where to point his gun.

Carly took that split second to fire.

She shot the man in the thigh. His gun flew out of his hand as he let out a yelp of pain and fell to the floor.

Carly yanked out her handcuffs and ran toward him. In an instant, she had him cuffed and lying helpless.

"Don't you move a muscle," she warned the handcuffed man. "I'll shoot you again if I have to."

She left him there and turned toward Lyle. Nancy Ruhl was already bending over her felled partner.

"He seems to be drugged," Nancy said.

Carly felt panic sweeping over her. The victims had been drugged with a paralyzing substance.

But she saw that Lyle wasn't completely unconscious. He was struggling to prop himself up with one arm and his lips were moving.

"He's saying some pretty weird stuff," Nancy told her.

Weird stuff? Carly wondered. She bent closer over Lyle and listened to him as he murmured a few words.

“Women … apes and monkeys … nothing but animals … not even the same species …”

Carly laughed aloud. She immediately understood that her partner had been playing mind games with the killer, stalling for time, pretending to be a like-minded woman-hater, and part of him was still doing that.

Carly stroked his hair and said, “It’s OK, Lyle. It’s over. You don’t have to act like a misogynous jerk anymore. You got a dose of something, didn’t you? Was it chloroform?”

“Vecuronium.”

“Well, you’ll be all right. We’ll get you to a hospital right away.”

“OK.”

“I’d better read this jerk his rights,” she grumbled, turning back to the moaning killer.

She had just done that when they all heard the sound of sirens wailing outside.

Nancy gasped aloud and said, “Wow, the cops are getting here just in time to save our lives!”

Both women burst into almost hysterical laughter.

CHAPTER THIRTY FIVE

Stop worrying, Carly told herself.

Sitting in the hospital waiting for Lyle to be released, she knew that she hadn't shaken off the stress and anxiety that went along with closing a murder case. It was hard to get out of an obsessive problem-solving mode.

Lyle is going to be his old self again, she thought.

When she'd visited him last night, he'd still been a bit delirious from the debilitating but nonfatal dose of vecuronium Derek Kuchan had injected into his neck back in the factory. The doctors had told them Lyle was lucky the dose was only partial, and that it hadn't been injected into an artery.

They insisted he just needed to rest now.

She looked at her watch. The BAU plane would be waiting at the Albuquerque Airport. Although they'd both arrived here on commercial flights, the private plane would fly them back to Quantico.

But will he really be up for the trip? she wondered.

She wondered if she'd been wrong to request the plane so soon. But Lyle had sharply insisted on it last night.

"You've got to get me the hell out of here," he'd told her. *"And I don't mean just this hospital. I mean this town."*

But now Carly wasn't sure that either Lyle's judgment or her own had been quite sound.

At least she knew the woman they had rescued was doing fine. Her injuries were superficial, and she seemed to be regaining emotional stability. Carly smiled as she remembered Nancy Ruhl yelling at Kuchan to distract him from shooting Lyle or her. That killer had picked a tougher woman than he'd realized.

So, she asked herself, *why are you still looking for things to worry about?*

Then Carly realized there was one bit of unfinished business that still nagged at her. She remembered the last time she'd heard from the spirit of Shane Crawford's dead sister, Bonnie. It was only then that the suicidal spirit had revealed to Carly the real reason she'd reached out. She wanted Carly's help to stop her brother from killing himself, like she had done. Bonnie's spirit wanted Shane to know that she was watching over him, and that she wanted him to live.

Carly remembered replying silently, *"I don't know how I can help."*

And the truth was, Carly still didn't know how to help. Right now, Shane Crawford was in a jail cell, and although Carly wasn't going to press assault charges against him, he was awaiting trial for obstruction of justice, and he'd doubtless face some well-deserved legal penalty. Carly couldn't very well just pay him a visit and tell him outright …

"By the way, I talked to your dead sister ..."

No, saying that to him face to face just wasn't an option.

But maybe ...

Another way to convey the message occurred to her. She took out her pen and notepad and thought about what to write to him. It had to be anonymous, of course—she couldn't let him know that one of the FBI agents who had caught him had been talking with the dead.

Most of all, the message had to be persuasive.

A tall order.

She began writing …

Shane, it doesn't matter who I am.

I just want you to know that your sister reached out to me from the other side.

She's afraid you feel responsible for her death.

She doesn't want you to take your own life.

She wants you to live.

Carly read over the message a few times. It seemed good that it was so simple. But nothing here seemed likely to convince Shane of the truth of the message.

How can I do that?

Then Carly flashed back to something else the spirit had said.

"I want him to live—like we always said to each other when I was alive, and we were kids ..."

And the phrase Bonnie and her brother had shared rattled through Carly's mind.

She wrote down a concluding sentence.

Bonnie wants you to "stay in the game."

She smiled as she imagined Shane's reaction to those four words—*"stay in the game."*

At least it will make him wonder, Carly thought.

It should make him think twice before doing himself harm.

She folded up the note and put it in her purse. At the airport she would put it in a stamped envelope and send it to Shane in jail.

She murmured aloud to Bonnie's spirit.

"I hope that helps."

She had no idea whether Bonnie heard her.

Just then she heard a familiar voice barking out from behind a pair of swing doors.

"Let me out of this damn thing right this minute!"

The doors swung open, and Carly saw her partner fully dressed and seated in a wheelchair, which was being pushed by an orderly.

"I can walk on my own, damn it!" Lyle snarled at the orderly.

"Be my guest," the orderly said with a note of good-natured impatience. "But not until we get you outside, where the hospital won't be legally responsible if you fall down and break your neck."

"So you just don't want to get sued," Lyle said.

"You got it," the orderly agreed cheerfully.

Carly hurried over to Lyle and gave him a kiss on the head. She followed as the orderly pushed the wheelchair down a hallway and out through automatic doors into the morning daylight.

As she helped Lyle out of the wheelchair, she noticed that he was using a cane.

"Are you still having trouble walking?" she asked him.

Lyle waved the cane at her and replied, "Naw, this is just an affectation. A style statement. Do you think it's a good look for me?"

"Very cool," Carly replied.

But she could see that Lyle was leaning on the cane. He needed the support, at least at the moment.

He'll get better soon, she thought.

They got into their borrowed vehicle, and Carly started to drive them out of Teapa on their way to the Albuquerque airport. After a few moments of silence, Lyle spoke.

"That was some pretty good work you did yesterday. Saving my life, I mean, and catching the killer. Did I happen to mention it yesterday?"

Carly chuckled and told him, "I don't mind hearing it again. And I did have some help from Nancy Ruhl."

"Oh, yeah—his intended victim."

"Right. She led me right to you. And she distracted him so I could get a good shot at his thigh."

"Well, the two of you taught that crazy misogynist a thing or two about women."

"That's probably too much to hope for."

Indeed, she knew that Derek Kuchan's pathology could never be cured without years and years of therapy, if such a thing was even possible. She wondered whether he'd get that kind of treatment in prison.

She also wondered how many men out there suffered from the same diseased hatred. Living in a world with stronger and stronger women seemed to be provoking such wounded men to increasingly frequent acts of violence.

We're liable to have other cases like this, she realized.

And she and Lyle had no choice but to deal with them one at a time. Meanwhile, she felt grateful to have men like Lyle in her life—men who respected and were unafraid of a strong woman like herself.

Another silence fell until Lyle spoke again, this time in a tired, sad voice.

"I'm getting old, Carly."

Carly felt a lump of emotion in her throat. Of course, she knew it was true. He wasn't even 60 yet, but he was old for an active agent. Lyle couldn't live this kind of life forever. But she'd never heard him admit it before.

She turned to look at him and saw that his broad, dark features did appear more exhausted than usual after a case. And was it her imagination, or did she see a few new gray hairs on his head?

"You've got plenty of years left," Carly said.

Those words sound so lame, she thought, her eyes moistening a little.

"You bet I do," Lyle growled defiantly. "I've got lots of years. And I've got a strong sense of purpose in life. Without this job, I'd hit the bottle again in no time. I'd die without this job. And if I ever talk about retirement, slap me silly. If you can't talk me out of it, take out that Glock of yours and shoot me."

Carly was startled.

"You know I'd never do that," she said.

"You wouldn't, huh? What the hell kind of partner are you?"

She knew Lyle was joking, but at the moment she wasn't amused by his humor.

She said, "The kind of partner who would take a bullet for you, the same as you'd do for me."

That shut Lyle up. Carly saw him staring out the side window.

Then she added, "And don't you forget it."

"I won't."

They didn't talk any more during most of the drive. But Carly couldn't stop worrying.

And I'm not the only one who worries about him, she thought.

She remembered that mysterious presence that had reached out to her when Lyle's life was at stake, and Carly had felt ready to sacrifice her own to save his. She remembered the spirit's words.

"I can't help him anymore. It's up to you to be there for him ... always."

She wondered—who was the spirit that cared so much for Lyle, even from the beyond?

She had no idea. All she knew was that she was receiving messages more frequently, with greater intensity, and from a growing number of spirits. Maybe that was because she needed more of their help in the life she led. Her gift—if that was the right word—was becoming more powerful.

And the more powerful it gets, the less I seem to understand it.

CHAPTER THIRTY SIX

It's good to be home, Carly thought as she stepped through her apartment door and set down her suitcase. It didn't bother her to be alone in this sprawling complex in Glensted, Virginia, where nobody had any idea who she was or what she did.

She relished her privacy.

Especially after such a demanding case, Carly really needed some downtime by herself. Lyle would be on leave for a while, and she could even take a day or two off. So she wasn't entirely pleased when her phone rang—at least not until she saw the caller's name.

Mark Lawson.

The last time they'd spoken on the phone, just before she'd flown out to New Mexico, he'd said, *"Let's not be strangers."*

Now it seemed that he'd meant it.

"Hi, Carly," Mark said in a shy voice when she answered.

"Hi, Mark. It's nice to hear your voice."

"It's nice to hear *your* voice. I saw on the news something about a serial killer in New Mexico. Was that your case?"

"It was. It's over now. I'm back home."

"Are you OK?"

"Sure."

"I'm glad. I hope you weren't in any serious danger."

Carly couldn't help rolling her eyes.

"Oh, no danger at all."

But she'd failed to keep a telltale note of irony out of her voice. And surely Mark could have detected that.

Then she admitted, "It was a tough case, Mark. And scary too. I'm fine, but I'm awfully tired. The truth is, I just got back to my apartment and …"

"I understand, and I won't keep you. I just wanted to let you know—I'm flying out to Washington in a couple of days for what I like to call a 'shyster convention.' I'll be in town for a week or so. I was wondering if we might be able to get together."

Carly felt a smile stretch across her face.

"I'd like that a lot," she said.

"Are you sure you'll feel up to it?"

"Definitely. I'll look forward to it."

"I'll get back to you about details. See you soon."

She felt warm all over as they ended the call. She found herself remembering those sweet evenings when she and Mark would sit on the porch swing of her childhood home, dreaming aloud of a wonderful future together.

It seems like such a long time ago, she thought.

But now she wondered—were new possibilities opening up for them?

Again, she found it hard to imagine a special agent of the FBI and a small-time lawyer winding up together.

But still ...

After her experience with a woman-hating psychopath, a sensitive, empathetic, intelligent, and responsible man like Mark seemed very attractive right now.

We'll just have to wait and see, she told herself.

Meanwhile, it really did feel good to be alone in this simply furnished living room which had so few decorations except for some trinkets and mementoes on her bookcase. One item among them caught her eye—the last picture she had of herself and Megan before her sister's disappearance. In it she and Megan were happily eating cotton candy at a carnival together.

Mark took that picture, she remembered.

Which reminded her—she'd brought home another item to add to that shelf. She opened up her suitcase and took out her sister's most treasured possession—the water globe with the two frolicking dolphins inside. She remembered the hours Megan had passed staring into that globe.

"It's my secret place," Megan had often said.

The bubbles whirled like a merry-go-round. Instead of setting the globe on the shelf, Carly sat down on her sofa and stared into its magical world.

"Where are you, Megan?" she asked.

Just then Carly heard a child's voice speaking out of the air.

"Carly ... Carly ... Are you there?"

Carly recognized the voice with a gasp. It wasn't Megan. It was Carly's childhood friend Tyler, who had been cruelly murdered so many years ago. Tyler's spirit had visited her once before to show her an image of Megan standing on a beach—apparently alive.

Carly remembered trying to reach out again to Tyler's spirit several days ago in Megan's room.

"Tyler, can you hear me?" she'd murmured aloud. *"Can you help me find Megan?"*

He hadn't spoken to her then. And since then, she'd been completely caught up in communications with spirits who'd helped her with the case.

But he was speaking to her now.

"I'm here," she whispered in a trembling voice. "I'm listening."

"I've got something else to show you."

Suddenly Carly's vision was filled by an ocean scene. She was looking across rough waters. Near the horizon was a line of jagged islands. She saw a high, sharply pointed central peak, and smaller ones surrounding it. Dolphins were leaping out of the waves nearby.

Carly realized the scene was actually a childhood memory.

Megan and I were on a boat together, she thought. *We were young, both still in elementary school.*

But where had they been?

She struggled to place that scene. It had something to do with her sister's love of dolphins.

Carly remembered that Mom and Dad had once taken them to a dolphin park where the creatures performed for an audience. They'd thought Megan would especially enjoy it. Instead, Megan had been sad to see her favorite creatures in captivity.

But one summer, Mom and Dad had taken them on vacation to California where they'd gone on a tour boat trip for whale watching.

I'm back there again, Carly realized, feeling the roughness of the water and cold spray of the waves.

And she could see her sister clapping her hands with joy.

"Oh, the dolphins!" Megan shouted. *"Look at the dolphins."*

And now Carly remembered something about those peaks rising out of the waves in the distance. It was one of a group of islands—a marine sanctuary that was closed to the public, inhabited only by scientific researchers.

Her heart beat faster and her breath quickened.

"Is she there, Tyler? Is Megan on one of those islands?"

But Tyler didn't reply, and the image faded.

And with a sinking heart, Carly remembered what Native Americans had called the place she'd just seen …

"Islands of the Dead."

NOW AVAILABLE!

NO WAY HOME
(A Carly See FBI Suspense Thriller—Book 3)

In a macabre and bizarre pattern, women grieving for their loved ones are turning up murdered themselves, targeted by a serial killer. FBI Special Agent Carly See will have to descend into a world of death to enter the killer's mind—and save the next victim before it's too late.

NO WAY HOME (A Carly See Suspense Thriller) is book #3 in a chilling new series by mystery and suspense author Rylie Dark, which begins with NO WAY OUT (book #1).

FBI Special Agent Carly See, a star in the elite BAU unit, hides a terrible secret: she can speak with the dead. The murder of her sister, still unsolved, plunged her life into grief and awakened a new power within her. All of it feels like a curse—until Carly realizes she can harness her new skills to solve cases. But her abilities are unreliable, and Carly must use her brilliant mind to complete the puzzle—all while struggling to keep her secret from her colleagues.

This killer, though, is always one step ahead, and Carly herself, leading the investigation, may not be as safe as she seems. In this game of cat and mouse, it will be a race to figure out what these victims have in common—and who is next on the killer's list.

But will Carly's vision lead her astray?

A page-turning thriller packed with twists and turns, secrets, and harrowing surprises you won't see the CARLY SEE series is a mystery series that will have you on the edge of your seat, endearing you to a brilliant and unique new character and having you turning pages, bleary-eyed, late into the night.

Books #4-#6—NO WAY LEFT, NO WAY UP, and NO WAY TO DIE—are now also available.

Rylie Dark

Bestselling author Rylie Dark is author of the SADIE PRICE FBI SUSPENSE THRILLER series, comprising six books (and counting); the MIA NORTH FBI SUSPENSE THRILLER series, comprising six books (and counting); the CARLY SEE FBI SUSPENSE THRILLER, comprising six books (and counting); and the MORGAN STARK FBI SUSPENSE THRILLER, comprising three books (and counting).

An avid reader and lifelong fan of the mystery and thriller genres, Rylie loves to hear from you, so please feel free to visit www.ryliedark.com to learn more and stay in touch.

BOOKS BY RYLIE DARK

SADIE PRICE FBI SUSPENSE THRILLER
ONLY MURDER (Book #1)
ONLY RAGE (Book #2)
ONLY HIS (Book #3)
ONLY ONCE (Book #4)
ONLY SPITE (Book #5)
ONLY MADNESS (Book #6)

MIA NORTH FBI SUSPENSE THRILLER
SEE HER RUN (Book #1)
SEE HER HIDE (Book #2)
SEE HER SCREAM (Book #3)
SEE HER VANISH (Book #4)
SEE HER GONE (Book #5)
SEE HER DEAD (Book #6)

CARLY SEE FBI SUSPENSE THRILLER
NO WAY OUT (Book #1)
NO WAY BACK (Book #2)
NO WAY HOME (Book #3)
NO WAY LEFT (Book #4)
NO WAY UP (Book #5)
NO WAY TO DIE (Book #6)

MORGAN STARK FBI SUSPENSE THRILLER
TOO LATE (Book #1)
TOO CLOSE (Book #2)
TOO FAR GONE (Book #3)

www.ingramcontent.com/pod-product-compliance
Lightning Source LLC
Chambersburg PA
CBHW030617310726
48979CB00003B/758

* 9 7 8 1 0 9 4 3 9 4 5 7 2 *